INFERNAL
BARGAIN

SELINA BEVAN

Cover Design by: Leigh Cover Designs

Editing by Dayna Hart

ISBN: 978-1-916719-80-4

AUTHOR NOTE

Please, please, please read the content advisories on my website before continuing.

I don't consider this book dark by any means BUT there are themes that run through the book that may be disturbing to some. Please look after yourself.

Hopefully, the blurb gave you an insight into what to expect, but if you flick to the back of this book, you'll find a content advisories page.

Lastly, please note that I am **British** and this book is written in **British English**. There are variations in the language between the US and British English.

Happy Reading!

Selina

CHAPTER ONE

BRONWYN

Add one vial of white dragon blood, three kelpie scales, a gryphon's wing, and one khepri (dried will work, though live is preferred) to the cauldron.

A sensible person would take one look at that ingredient list and back away.

Fortunately, or not, depending on who you asked, sense abandoned me long ago, and since my grandmother died two weeks ago, I had nothing left to lose. No family, no friends, no coven, and no fucks to give. It was a dangerous place for a witch.

The lines between black and white blurred far too

easily when you had nothing to live for and as much as that scared me, being alone forever scared me more.

Which is why I stood here, in my grandmother's dining room staring at the inverted pentagram I'd painstakingly drawn on the floor using chicken blood, bowls of each ingredient placed at the points. It must have taken a sick witch to equate these creatures with cardinal points, but who was I to argue if the damn spell worked?

Your common witch wouldn't touch this spell with a bargepole. Not just because it was written in some long-lost language and a right bitch to translate, but most would laugh at the notion of sourcing any of those things.

I mean, first you needed to find them, and these creatures had abandoned our realm long ago. If any remained, they were few and far between.

Now, assume you could find a kelpie.

Catch it at the right time and they'd hand over a few scales without pause. But the wrong time? It would drag you to a watery death.

Did that stop me spending days translating the spell and tapping every black market connection I had left? Of course not.

If it were easy to summon the devil, everyone would do it.

For a second, the enormity of it threatened to overwhelm me. It swirled inside of me, merging with the heavy ball of grief that sat just beneath my solar plexus. My eyes burned, tears threatening to sap away my strength right when I needed it.

The faster you do this, the sooner you get her back.

I shut my eyes and breathed deep, willing all my emotions into a cage in the back of my mind. It would only work temporarily, so I needed to get the show on the road fast.

I counted to three and released the breath, allowing it to balance me. Then I opened the grimoire and set to work, my tongue tripping over the Old Tuathic words.

"I, daughter of night, summon you, King of Sins, the rebellious angel of death. Bring me counsel, bring me sight, bring me light. I have a bargain for thee, Lucifer Morningstar…"

The air crackled around me as I continued, invoking the four corners and repeating the words in English, Latin and Welsh to be sure I'd left no stone unturned.

When the words ran out, I raised my silver athame to my palm. For a brief second, doubt flickered to life in my mind. Not because I was summoning the Devil. Oh no. Because the book very specifically demanded I cut my palm.

Ordinarily, I was the girl heckling the TV when some idiotic teen witch sliced up the most painful and difficult place on her body to heal. The forearm produces just as much blood and heals faster because you're not constantly using it.

At that moment, I probably should have stopped and questioned my sanity. Doubt over the placement of a blood sacrifice. Pfft. I mean come on.

I took another deep breath and slashed the blade across my palm. Blood pooled thick and fast. I held my hand out, just over the salt lines surrounding the pentagram and let my blood fall.

It splattered against the old hardwood floors, fizzling and smoking. If my grandmother could see me now, she'd be scowling. She loved these floors, but if I had to pay a price to get her back, she could deal with refinishing the damaged—

The candles flared, the flame shooting up two feet and scaring the life out of me. The air shimmered again, almost solidifying around the pentagram. It engulfed my wrist, still held over the circle, the blood slowing to a trickle.

I snatched my hand to my chest and backed away. The pressure in the room intensified.

In the centre of the circle, sickly shades of colour swirled, blacks, reds and greens mingling together until a ball formed. Everything went still around me, and for a second, I couldn't draw breath, like the air had been sucked out of the room.

Boom!

The ball shattered. Air rushed out of the circle, blowing out the candles. It swirled around me, creating a vortex of some sort with the dust that had gathered since my grandmother's death. Heart pounding, I covered my eyes before something could blind me.

"Isn't this a surprise," a bored yet amused voice said, the sound so deep and filled with power I could have sworn it caressed my face. I stiffened my spine, fighting off the shiver desperately clamouring to get out. When I opened my eyes, all I could do was stare.

I'd done it.

I'd really fucking done it.

In the middle of my pentagram stood a towering figure draped in a perfectly tailored black suit. His long, dirty-blond hair was pulled back and secured at his neck. But damn, those eyes! Bluer and deeper than any ocean, pulling me into their depths. His gaze roamed around the room, taking in the empty, desolate space. "Did the rest of your coven desert you? Never mind, I'll hunt them down later. But you? You're going to regret this, little witch. Now, hand me the grimoire, and I won't kill you for summoning me," he said, his voice low and enticing. His pupils expanded, and the power in the room amped up.

His voice made my nerve-endings sing, his power stroked my skin. Well, that was just freaky, and he needed to stop.

His smirk disintegrated as my attention shifted to the wings unfurling from his back. They spread out, each one twice as long as Lucifer was tall. I stared in awe, my mouth dropping open slightly. The feathers gleamed like black opals, glossy and iridescent in the candlelight. As he flexed them, the wings stirred the air around us into a gentle breeze.

"Are those real?" My head tilted to the side, studying them.

The power froze in its attempts to manhandle me.

His eyes narrowed as he considered me, a sinister smile curling his lips. "Well, this just got interesting."

Unable to stop myself, I reached a hand up, fingers outstretched to touch those impossibly soft-looking feathers. But at the last second, I caught myself, snatching my hand back. The summoning circle glowed faintly, reminding me of the consequences should I break it — I would release Lucifer into this world and he would definitely kill me first.

He watched me closely, an amused but devious glint in his eyes.

"I want to make a deal."

He sighed. "Of course, you do. You mortals are all alike." He folded his arms across his broad chest and retracted his power, spearing me with those eyes again. I bit my tongue before I could demand he give it back. "Get on with it. I don't have all day."

"I want my grandmother back."

He cocked his head to the side. "And you think I have her?"

I nodded. "You're the Devil. She's a witch. I know you do."

Lucifer chuckled. "I'm flattered, petal, but there are infinite divisions of Hell. I am but one overlord. Your grandmother could be in any one of them."

The confidence I'd built up to face him disintegrated. It took all of my strength not to let my shoulders slump in defeat. Any sign of weakness in front of this man — being — could spell my death.

If he didn't have her, I'd wasted all of this time and money to summon him for nothing. There wasn't a spell in the book for summoning the other lords. It didn't mention others. Fuck.

"Don't look so sad. I didn't say I couldn't help, just that I don't know where she is." His amusement danced around me, bolstering my spirits in a way I couldn't understand.

"Then how?"

"You're clearly a talented witch." Something sparkled in his eyes, there and gone in a blink. "I can't bring her to you, but you could… with the right spell."

My eyes narrowed. "And you have such a spell?"

He nodded, his lips curling. "For a price, of course."

"Of course," I muttered, my tone dry. "Name your price, Devil."

Lucifer studied me clinically, his gaze raking me from head to toe as he appeared to weigh his options. His power returned, poking and prodding me in delightful ways.

"Your firstborn child," he finally said with a gravitas only the Devil could achieve.

I snorted. "That's a bit cliché, isn't it?"

He smirked again. "It is, but that doesn't change my terms."

A thread of excitement shot through me at his serious tone. It almost seemed too easy. Just give up something I never intended to have. And I'd get my grandmother back… Well, get the spell to get her back but what was one more step when I'd already come so far?

"You have a deal."

He shook his head, almost like he didn't want to do it. "Very well, witch."

He clicked his fingers, and a pop sounded. A leather parchment and a black-feathered quill appeared. Light blazed across it, words written in cursive lettering so small I squinted to make out my name.

I hadn't told him my name.

"Did you think you could summon me without me knowing who you were?" He laughed as my brow furrowed. "Oh, that is priceless. You Owen women are all the same, deluded into these ridiculous ideas of grandeur. As if you could ever successfully hide yourselves from the Devil."

Why would my ancestors worry about hiding themselves from the Devil?

It doesn't matter now. Sign the damn thing and get the spell.

I plucked the quill from the air. Lucifer flicked his finger, and the cut in my palm started bleeding again.

For a second, all I could do was stare at it, the idea of signing a contract in my own blood abhorrent for some reason.

I'd just spilled a ton of it all over the floor to feed the summoning.

Scoffing at myself, I dipped the quill's tip in my cut and signed.

CHAPTER TWO

LUCIFER

*T*he contract burned away in a flash of flame, leaving behind a scroll. It floated in front of the red-haired witch, patiently waiting for her to reach out and take it.

For over two hundred years, no Owen witch had dared to summon me, let alone make a bargain. They knew better. But those witches didn't let their emotions leak, either. This one lacked the finesse I was used to from her ancestors.

Oh well. All the better to appease the council before they took matters into their own hands.

The witch, Bronwyn, snatched the scroll out of the

air and hugged it to her chest. She grinned at me from the other side of her useless salt line, her excitement overpowering the nauseating grief emanating from every pore. Her grey eyes sparkled with it.

Really, when would these witches learn? No power in the world could confine me. Not even The Morrigan's veil, protecting the human world from the old gods, could touch the Underworld as it had intended to do.

When she'd sacrificed her twelve warriors, all the doors were supposed to close. Instead, her witches got trapped and most of the old gods were confined to their realm.

No, little Bronwyn couldn't control me with a salt line and her barely tapped power — she needed far more.

She was a comely thing, I supposed, with fiery waves of copper hair cascading over her shoulder. Pleasant enough features on her heart-shaped face, though that wicked smirk, both tempting and trouble-stirring, whispered of the bedlam she could unleash if given half the chance.

Not that the council cared one bit what the last Owen witch looked like. All they cared about was balance. Specifically, returning balance to the world now that the old gods had left a void the rest of us stood no chance of filling alone. We needed to pull more power from the core, and to do that, there needed to be more of us.

She had more guts than sense, that much was clear. Possibly a good thing considering the fate she'd signed herself to. A pleased glint in those stormy eyes betrayed her youth and inexperience. She couldn't have seen more than thirty mortal years.

"Good thing I never wanted kids," she thought, failing to so much as smother her thoughts or try to shield them.

Really, had these witches fallen so far from their roots they had forgotten everything that had made them feared among demonkind?

What a shame.

Bronwyn chuckled while reading through the spell. She truly believed she had outsmarted the devil.

Now it was my turn to grin.

My power surged forward, reaching for her as it had when she'd first summoned me.

A trickle of unease slithered through her mind and she glanced up, meeting my gaze with one of confusion.

"Didn't your grandmother teach you anything about dealing with the Devil?" My grin widened as her pulse raced. That would be a no. "Read the fucking fine print."

I stepped towards her, through the magic surrounding her summoning circle and over the pointless salt line. Her eyes widened and she scrambled away with a squeal, hitting a wall of power she clearly hadn't sensed. The contract burst back into being before me and I snatched it up, smudging the velum. The ancient thing hissed its displeasure in my mind, but I paid it no attention.

"What does that say, witch?"

"That — that I give you my firstborn child," she said, her voice shaking. Then her gaze hardened along with her voice. "Like we agreed."

I chuckled, and a flare of annoyance speared through her, making energy swirl in her eyes.

"Read. It. Now."

I shoved the contract at her, holding the end of it up so that she couldn't do anything but stare at the tiny letters appending the contract.

Her eyes widened and I sighed. Idiotic mortals. "Read it aloud. Prove to me that you actually understand this time."

"In exchange for the aforementioned services, the female party consents to conceive and deliver into this world the blood-child of Lucifer Morningstar…" Her voice rose on my name, and her panicked gaze clashed with mine. "You can't be serious."

"Keep reading."

"Within thirteen nights of the pact fulfilment, or upon successful conception, whichever comes first." Her face paled. "That seems extreme. What if I can't even have children?"

"Keep reading." Boredom coloured my tone.

"Should conception not occur naturally within the allotted span, the female party hereby agrees to undergo any and all magical treatments prescribed by Lucifer Morningstar or his appointed physicians to induce or enable pregnancy. Refusal to comply will be counted as a breach of contract."

Pure unadulterated fury claimed her features. She thrashed against the power holding her still, calling me every insult imaginable. It impressed me for a tick of the clock but I'd rather not be in the mortal plane when the lust spell kicked in.

I sighed. "Since you refuse to follow instructions, I'll help you." I turned the contract to face me and read the final lines. "The resultant child, begat of the Morningstar, shall upon birth be relinquished to the custody and authority of the Dark Lord exclusively until the end of days."

"Why the hell would you want an innocent child?"

I snorted. "No child of mine would be innocent, petal. Use your head."

She clamped her lips shut. Maybe there would be hope for her yet.

"By signing in blood freely given, this covenant is sealed beyond all contestation across all planes of existence — material, spiritual, infernal, and otherwise. These are the irrefutable conditions of our arrangement herein." I threw the hissing contract over my head and willed a portal to open, sending the disgruntled thing back to Hell where it belonged. "So, Bronwyn Owen, are you going to willingly fulfil the terms of our infernal bargain, or are you going to make this difficult on us both?"

Her eyes flashed silver. "What are you going to do, make me?" she spat, outrage etching lines in her face.

I sighed, barely refraining from rolling my eyes. "You misunderstand, little witch. The magics binding our arrangement care not for what either of us desires. They will run their course with or without your... cooperation."

I held her gaze, watching the implication sink in as those stormy eyes widened. "The only question is whether we reach the inevitable outcome in hours"—I trailed a suggestive finger down her rapidly paling cheek—"or days."

Silence reigned but for her thrumming pulse. The gears turned behind her eyes as she glowered at me.

Oh, how I hoped she would test me. How long had it been since a mere mortal sparked more than cruel amusement within me? I schooled my features to stillness, refusing to betray my growing excitement.

A clock ticked in the next room, its grinding cogs loud in the silence that descended. I waited with diminishing patience, longer than I should have. For at least two centuries, this contract had waited for an Owen witch to call me. The rest of them had been too sensible. Their ancestors had warned them what would happen should they bargain with me.

Why The Morrigan mandated that the child be of Owen blood, I hadn't asked. It mattered little to me. But the longer I watched them, pushing themselves to the brink of extinction, the more concerned I'd grown.

What would happen if I didn't produce an heir to the Infernal Throne? Would my kingdom lose power? Become overwhelmed?

I had contemplated drawing more from the core. One more council meeting, and I might have tried.

Now it didn't matter.

This one had signed the contract and she was mine.

"Well, witch?" I forced through my clenched jaw when I couldn't bear to wait any more. "What shall it be?"

She rocked back on her heels, her eyes almost

rolling back in her head. "What the…" Her face paled and her eyes narrowed on me. "What's happening to me?"

"The Morrigan embedded a failsafe into the contract." My grin turned feral as I pulled her flush against me. "When you signed, you triggered the lust spell."

She stared at me, dawning horror spreading across her face. "Lust spell?"

"Yes. By signing the contract, you've cursed us both to thirteen days and nights of this madness." I caressed her jaw, the spell beginning to burn through my veins.

Unconsciously, she tilted her head, chasing my touch.

"Our bargain. His heir. I had to…" her stilted thoughts echoed inside my mind, serving as an early warning system.

She tried to shove me back, but I had already tightened my grip.

"This isn't me. Isn't real. Just magic, twisting my will."

My fingers trailed down her neck, leaving a blazing trail over her fevered skin. Her breath came faster, desire and panic building inside of her.

"Shh, relax." I stroked a hand down her back soothingly. She trembled, but her body leaned into me. I gently grasped her chin, tipping her face up. "I know you're frightened. But we're both trapped in this spell now. Fighting will only bring you pain."

"I don't—"

"Let go, Bronwyn. Allow yourself to feel it. The magic won't be denied."

I lowered my head towards hers. Against her will, her lips parted in anticipation.

At the first brush of my lips against hers, unwanted pleasure cascaded through us. Electricity zinged through me as her hands slid up my chest. My heart raced impossibly as her fingers tangled in my hair, intensifying the heat between us.

With my last ounce of control, I opened a portal and dragged her through it. She whimpered once but barely seemed to notice the rollercoaster rush of power around us, her lips never left mine.

It had been aeons since I had experienced anything like this. It was intoxicating, a dance of temptation. Any thought of resisting the spell evaporated from my mind. I could only revel in the sinful feeling of it all.

Who knew a kiss could feel like a brand?

CHAPTER THREE

BRONWYN

*T*he portal spat us out somewhere. I didn't care enough to break the kiss. Not even my spinning head or flip-flopping stomach could convince me.

Lucifer deepened the kiss. His hands glided over me, skilled and coaxing. My resistance wavered beneath that drugging touch. The spell unfurled inside me, burning deliciously as it invaded my bloodstream. What choice did I have but to surrender?

He groaned into the kiss, his grip tightening. We stumbled back until my shoulders hit the cold stone. His unyielding body pinned mine to the wall.

Sensing my crumbling defences, he lifted his head, capturing my gaze. "That's it, petal," he growled, his voice rough with desire. "Give yourself to me. I'll make it good for you, I promise."

I did. I couldn't help it.

I wanted him, needed him too badly.

On some level, I knew I should keep refusing him. This was wrong. I didn't want it. But the spell surged through me, blotting out all reason and leaving no room for reluctance. The desire pulsing through me with every caress and press of his body against mine drowned all rational thought.

There was only Lucifer's addictive touch, his hard body moulded perfectly to mine. The rest faded into hazy insignificance.

I let go of all restraint, allowing myself to be consumed by the fiery desire that coursed through my veins. My hands, no longer under my control, reached out to him, craving the pleasure that only he could give. His firm muscles flexed as I dragged my fingertips over them, and I couldn't help but moan into his mouth.

The fabric of his shirt gave way beneath my fingertips as I unbuttoned it eagerly, desperate to feel his bare skin against mine.

My body was on fire for him, and I couldn't control it.

His lips moved from mine, pressing open-mouthed kisses against my jaw and down my neck. His fingers danced along the curve of my spine, making my body arch toward him, seeking more.

The final button slipped free and I shoved and tugged at his shirt with a singular focus that made him chuckle in a way I never imagined the Devil would. He shrugged it off, revealing inch after inch of glorious muscle. His chest was blanketed in tattoos that came alive under the dim light of the room. Intricate designs twisted and turned, intertwining with one another as if telling a story only known to him.

His breath hitched as I traced my fingers over the inked lines, my nails grazing lightly over his hardened nipples. He stared at me, his pupils blown with lust, a feral hunger burning in their depths that matched the need roaring within me. With an animalistic growl, his lips crashed against mine in another searing kiss, his tongue duelling with mine.

I couldn't think straight.

All I could do was feel; the heat of his lips and the touch of his rough hands on my skin. He tasted like wine and sin, and I couldn't get enough. I forgot about everything but him and the way his fingers dug into my hips, pulling me against him.

He tore at my clothes with impatient hands, making

me tremble. With a frustrated huff, a surge of power shot out of him, tickling my skin. I moaned as it caressed me from head to toe, barely noticing when my favourite jeans dissolved into nothing.

His bare chest brushed against mine, and it was like an electric shock running through me. My nipples hardened and I gasped, arching into him.

My body screamed for more.

More kisses. More touches. More pleasure.

His hands roamed over my back, pushing my auburn hair aside to trail a path of scorching kisses down the column of my neck.

"Fuck." He groaned against my skin, making me shudder. "It shouldn't feel this good." His voice was raw with lust, and it sent shivers down my spine. "This isn't — We need to— Stop."

I gasped as he nipped at my earlobe, making me shift restlessly against him. "Don't stop," I begged, barely recognising my own voice beneath the desperation.

He chuckled darkly before pulling away, his eyes smouldering as he met my gaze. "If you say so."

Then his head descended again, only this time, his entire body followed. His tongue flicked over my skin, driving me wild. I held onto him, legs shaking as he kissed his way down, down, down...

He kneeled before me, placing himself at the perfect height to torture my breasts.

I let out a breathless whimper as he captured a nipple between his teeth, teasing it with a gentle nip before soothing it with his tongue, sucking the bud deep into his mouth. The sensation sent an electric jolt straight to the core of my being, igniting a wildfire of desire within me.

He kept teasing, flicking, and sucking, until I was a puddle of wanton desire. My knees shook, but he held me up, refusing to let me fall. And then he moved.

"Lucifer," I groaned, desperate for more. His hands travelled down my stomach, setting my skin on fire, until they skimmed my thighs.

He kissed my torso, moving down while I panted. He stopped to drag his teeth along my hipbone and I squirmed under his mouth, a moan catching in my throat. He glanced up, a wicked grin on his lips.

"Impatient?"

I nodded, biting my bottom lip and trying to keep quiet, but it was impossible. He chuckled, his breath ghosting over my opening.

His hands slid down my thighs, fingers dancing over my skin. My breath froze as he parted my folds, exposing me to him. He nuzzled against me, his hot breath sending shockwaves through my core, before slipping a finger inside.

I hissed when he removed it, replacing it with his tongue, tracing the seam of my pussy, before slipping the tip inside, teasing the entrance.

"More, please."

And he gave me more, more than I could handle. He fucked me with his fingers and tongue, feeding me first one, then two, then three digits. His fingers plunged deep, stretching me and filling me with blinding pleasure.

I cried out, my fingers tangling in his hair as he flicked and teased my clit in a way that defied human understanding.

My legs buckled under the onslaught of sensation, but he held me up. He braced me against the wall with his free hand, holding firm, keeping me from falling as he fucked my entrance with unrestrained abandon. It was almost too much.

The world spun as he licked, teased, and suckled, drowning me in pleasure.

I couldn't catch a breath.

"Please," I whimpered, my hips undulating against his face. "Please, I need—"

He looked up at me, his eyes hooded. "What do you

need, petal?" His voice was velvet and warm, a sinful promise.

I swallowed hard, trying to gather my thoughts. My heartbeat thrummed in my ears. I pressed my lips together, trying to hold the words in, but the spell was too strong.

"I need you," I whispered.

That devilish smile spread across his face. "Yes, you do," he murmured, his voice like honey dripping off his tongue.

Without giving me so much as a second to catch my breath, he stood, his hard length pressing against my stomach. He licked his lips, his eyes dark with desire.

"Say it," he commanded, looking down at me.

I bit my tongue, fighting my body's need to give him everything he wanted.

"I need you inside me," I panted, losing the battle while my body ached for release.

"Good girl." He smiled, no doubt sensing exactly what those words did to the final shreds of my resistance.

With a swift movement, he lifted me effortlessly, and I wrapped my legs around his waist. The cold stone grated against my back, providing a contrasting sensation to the scorching heat of Lucifer pressed against my front.

I clung to him, my nails digging into his sculpted back as he ravished my lips with fervour.

He thrust, a single movement that seated him deep inside me. I moaned at the invasion, my eyes widening in shock and pain.

But it was divine pain.

The feel of him stretching me, filling me... I'd experienced nothing like it. His power fizzed and crackled against me.

When he started to move, I could swear I went cross-eyed at the combined sensations. His dick had ridges or something, I swear. They rubbed against my walls, sending sparks of ecstasy through my body. And then something nudged my clit, sealing my descent into mindless pleasure. I couldn't figure out what it was but that nub caressed my most sensitive nerves with every thrust.

His hips pumped in a rhythm that matched my frantic pulse and I moaned, my voice raw and uncontrolled.

I clung to him, desperate for more, and yet afraid of the intensity. But he showed no mercy. His skin slick with sweat, he picked up the pace, driving into me harder and harder.

I could have imagined it but he seemed to tilt his hips to ensure the ridges caught that spot inside of me no man had managed to touch and the nub slapped against my clit. To say I was mindless would be an understatement. I could barely keep my eyes open under the onslaught of pleasure.

My nails dug into his shoulders, leaving marks some repressed part of me rejoiced in. The world around us melted away with each thrust, leaving only the fiery heat between us.

"Fuck," I cried, my body clenching around him.

He groaned in response, his face contorting in pleasure. He skimmed his palms down my body, teasing and pinching my nipples, sending shivers through me. His movements grew wilder, driving both of us harder against the wall.

"Mine," he growled against my ear. "You're mine." He slammed into me again, harder, filling me with his thick length.

A small voice tried to raise a protest at his claim. The words prodded at my mind, nagging at the partition the spell had placed between me and my inhibitions.

But the part of me that enjoyed seeing my marks on his skin shouted louder. She delighted in his claim, rolling around in the words like an absolute hussy.

I gasped at the intensity of the sensation, my body responding as my mind screamed for him to stop. But there was no escaping the dark lust that bound us together. The room spun as he pounded into me faster, our hips slapping together in a searching desperation. I arched my back, needing more of him — his touch, his possession.

"Please," I moaned, my voice ragged. "Let me come."

His teeth grazed my neck and liquid heat pooled in my core. "You will," he said, his voice low and rough.

I could feel it building inside me — the pressure, the need. His hips ground against me in a feral movement that forced that spur to pulse against my clit, sending off little sparks of pleasure that had my eyes practically rolling back in my head.

Fuck! It felt so good, so wrong, but I couldn't help myself.

The world around me blurred into a haze of ecstasy as Lucifer continued his relentless assault on my senses. Each thrust sent shockwaves rippling through me, igniting a fire that consumed every inch of my being.

His thrusts grew faster and more forceful, each one propelling me closer to the edge. Every nerve ending in my body was electrified, pulsating with an all-consuming need for release.

Lucifer's grip on my hips tightened, his fingers

digging into my flesh as he quickened his pace. The urgency in his movements grew, a primal hunger driving him to claim me completely. The sound of our bodies colliding echoed off the stone walls, mingling with our ragged breaths and desperate moans.

In the back of my mind, I started to worry that we had been cursed. The higher my body soared with no break, the more I worried that my orgasm would never come, that he had in fact dragged me to hell and doomed me to chase my release forever.

But then every muscle in my body tensed up. My inner walls tightened, clamping down on his cock until he grunted, his movements slowing as I fell over the edge and dragged him with me.

I screamed his name as I came undone in his arms, feeling him pump his seed into me. It was hot and thick, and pulsing with power. It blanketed me, and my body absorbed it greedily, sucking up every cast-off grain of energy, storing it away in places I hadn't realised existed.

CHAPTER FOUR

LUCIFER

I jolted awake, hissing through clenched teeth. My chest burned. Power flooded me, priming me to battle my foe. Only she was unreachable.

"Morrigan!" I roared to the heavens, uncaring if I woke the witch. "Take it back, you spineless bitch!"

"What's wrong?" Bronwyn cried beside me, confusion and fear rising her voice to a pitch the hellhounds would appreciate.

I scarcely heard her. I glared at the glowing violet sigil searing itself above my heart, melding itself far too seamlessly with my tattoos. The twin spiral, a mark I hadn't seen in more than three hundred years and would have been glad to never see again.

"You think to force my hand, witch goddess!" I roared at the ceiling, letting the burn of horror and rage wash over me.

The air crackled with the force of my fury. The coals leapt to life in the fireplace. Even the soft glow of the bedside lamps seemed to flicker in rhythm with my building wrath.

I threw back the covers and scrambled from the bed, ignoring the terrified look on Bronwyn's face. She'd have to get used to it. Especially now that meddling fucking bitch had bound us together.

I reached for the oppressive weight of the celestial bond, my hand instinctively clawing at the branded mark. I wrapped my power around it and tugged. It was fruitless and only sent pain stabbing through me.

A soulbond. She dared mark me with a fucking soulbond. Me! The King of Sins, the Lord of Darkness, marked like common cattle by an exiled goddess.

"Remove this bond at once, you duplicitous crone!" I bellowed, determined to make the wretched Goddess hear me somehow. "I gave you my word. I kept every condition of our pact. I did not agree to sign myself over to eternal enslavement!"

And it would be enslavement, living for eternity tied to a woman, any woman.

Bronwyn staggered as she climbed out of the bed, her hand going to her chest while her eyes widened. "What's happening to me?" she choked out, her panic a tang I could taste in the air.

The sight only darkened my mood.

"You go too far!" My voice thundered through the room; I was beyond fury now. I clawed at the brand on my skin, but its magic burrowed deeper.

The Morrigan, that insufferable goddess of manipulation, had orchestrated a game with stakes higher than she could pay. My fury intensified with every passing moment that the bond remained fixed, tying me to the Owen witch.

"Do you hear me, Morrigan?" I shouted, my words cutting through the thickening air like blades. "This treachery won't go unpunished. I will make you rue the day you dared to toy with the Morningstar!"

My words echoed around me, amplified by my power to deliver them to Ethereorium, the god realm.

"If you don't remove this binding, I will unleash hell upon you. Your barrier will not keep us out. I will shatter it, undoing all that you've worked for. No sanctuary will shelter you. I'll make the very cosmos tremble at the mention of your name!"

Breathing hard, I waited with all of my focus directed inward, watching the ribbon connecting our souls for the smallest sign of fraying or snapping. Seconds passed by and nothing happened.

The irony of my situation didn't escape me. The Devil, the embodiment of rebellion, trapped by the whims of a manipulative goddess.

My fury scorched the air around me in waves. My wings snapped open and my sword appeared. If I couldn't destroy the meddlesome goddess, I would just destroy everything else within my reach.

Including the witch.

With no more Owen witches left, she couldn't force another woman on me.

My vision was a blur of crimson. Sword raised, I dove for Bronwyn with a feral cry.

Shock widened her eyes. "What the hell are you doing?" she shrieked.

I ignored her, the relentless grip of anger propelling me forward. I swung the sword with all the force my supernatural strength could muster, aiming to sever the accursed bond. Yet, each strike met nothing but empty air as Bronwyn dodged with an unnatural agility for a mortal.

"Why are you doing this?" she asked, voice wavering, her confusion evolving into a mixture of fear and frustration. "Lucifer, stop!"

But I wouldn't. The weight of the soulbond felt like chains constraining my very essence.

Her gaze hardened, silver flames sparking in those storm-cloud eyes. Defiance burned in them now, chasing away her fear.

My next rushed attack met an invisible barrier, the clash reverberating down my sword arm. She began to channel her power, unwittingly tugging at something inside of me while she did it.

I bared sharp teeth, circling while she matched my steps warily. "You only delay the inevitable, little fool!"

Another blistering wave of power forced me back a step. The minx had claws, it seemed. But mine were longer, and my fury was endless.

With each swing, she blocked my strikes effortlessly, her movements a dance of elemental resistance.

"Why?" Her voice shifted, no longer a plea but a challenge. "You force me to see through our deal…" She blushed, swallowing hard as her gaze jumped to my bed and back to me. "And then kill me before I can complete it? How does that make sense?"

Her words only fuelled my fury. I fainted left, then struck right, faster than mortals could blink. Yet she sidestepped. The blade nicked the soft skin of her shoulder, and I howled as an identical burning slash seared through my own.

The cut on my shoulder revealed itself, deeper and more pronounced than the one I had inflicted on her.

"Gods be damned!" I bellowed at the ceiling and the exiled orchestrator of this farce. With a disgusted snarl, I dismissed my blade. If I couldn't take my fury out on the witch, then I needed a new outlet. One that could die.

The snap of my bedchamber door claimed my attention. I glanced over to find Bronwyn gone, nothing but her fear-laced scent and a trail of blood, spotted across the polished marble, staining the black rugs towards the door. The drops fizzled before my eyes as the palace absorbed them.

At first, fury spurred me to follow what was mine. To wring answers about this forced bonding from that delicate throat... among other things.

I took a step forward, intending to go after her. But then realisation struck. I was stuck with her in my palace for the next nine months — longer if I couldn't break The Morrigan's bond.

Frustration coiled within me. The situation was rapidly spiralling out of my control, a fact that deepened my annoyance. I needed a moment to gather my thoughts, to devise a plan for dealing with the

obstinate   witch   and   her   infuriatingly   resilient
soulbond.

My eyes swept across the room, the aftermath of
our clash scattered like the remnants of a hurricane-
force storm. The sigil had stopped glowing, settling into
a black ink that blended seamlessly with my tattoos.

It mocked me with its permanence.

The scent of burnt ozone lingered, a remnant of
our clash, mixing with the faint metallic tang of the
blood that had once stained the floor. The room, once a
haven of calculated elegance, now reeked of chaos and
the inexplicable bond that bound us.

With a snap of my fingers, I returned it to its orig-
inal state and turned my back on it, barely giving the
room a second look.

The little witch needed to learn to obey.

And what better way than letting her experience
the realities of the Infernal Throne, my palace, unpro-
tected? She might wear my scent, but it wouldn't be
strong enough to scare off my Demon Legions.
Bronwyn Owen would learn that in my realm, defiance
had dire consequences. It was time to show her the true
meaning of fear, a lesson that would be etched into her
soul for eternity.

CHAPTER FIVE

BRONWYN

*C*razy fucking Devil.

I tore down the stone corridor, my ragged breathing and pounding heartbeat echoing off the walls. Blood trickled between my fingers as I clutched my wounded arm, cursing the temperamental bastard.

And I was supposed to leave a kid with that raging psycho? As if!

Where the hell am I?

These creepy halls all looked the same. Gothic archways and towering obsidian columns whirled together.

I blinked sweat from my eyes as another wave of

that nasty sulphur stench hit me. Lungs burning, I choked down shallow breaths in the oppressive heat.

Glancing over my shoulder, paranoia gnawed at me. No sign of tall, blond, and psychotic yet. I half-expected him to be right on my tail, all flames and fury, his robes swishing dramatically.

The guy was so extra; it wouldn't be surprising.

Tricking me into a life-changing deal and then kidnapping me to a foreign world only to attack me with a freaking sword.

I mean, come on! Who the hell did he think he was?

No matter, I would escape him… once I found my way out of this maze of corridors.

So many turns, so many doors to nowhere. I tried a bunch and either found nothing but brick or absolute darkness. Why have so many of them if they went nowhere?

"Okay, Bron, you've officially outdone yourself," I muttered, my voice a mix of frustration and a touch of amusement at my predicament. "Lost in Hell. Bravo."

Panic gripped me as the gothic architecture of Lucifer's sprawling… palace, citadel, castle? What the hell was this place?

I took another turn, stumbling into a corridor that appeared narrower than the rest. The air grew thick with an unsettling crackle, and distant echoes reached my ears, making my skin crawl.

Then, an unearthly howl echoed down the corridor, sending shivers down my spine. I froze, heart pounding in my chest. The sound wasn't like anything I'd heard before – a mix of anguish and hunger.

Shadows moved in front of me, something big moving my way. Sharp claws skittered on stone, closer and closer.

Oh, no, no, no, not dealing with this crap!

I spun on my heel and ran. Fear tightened its grip on me. I glanced over my shoulder, expecting to see Lucifer, but it was something far worse.

A group of humanoid creatures, twisted and grotesque, rushed towards me. Their limbs bent at unnatural angles, and their eyes glowed with an otherworldly hunger. My brain struggled to make sense of their horrifying forms.

Demons. I was being chased by real fucking demons.

"Great. Just great!" I muttered to myself, my heart racing as I sprinted down the corridor. These things were fast, and Lucifer had already left me winded.

I risked a glance back, terror clawing at my throat. They were gaining on me, their nightmarish figures closing the gap. My breaths came in ragged gasps, and every muscle screamed in protest.

My pulse pounded in my ears as I pushed my aching body into an awkward sprint. A stairwell loomed on my left, blessedly free of the freak brigade. I banked towards it, yelping as claws grazed my arm, drawing fresh blood.

"Back off, Cujo!" I yelled, slamming the door shut. The heavy thud of bodies hitting the other side sent my heart into my throat. "This is *not* how I want to die! Do you hear me, Lucifer? If this is your idea of a joke, cut it out now!"

The door creaked under the pressure of them pounding against it, and I yelped. Heart pounding, I bolted up the narrow stairs. Behind me, the door cracked as bodies slammed against the solid oak.

Fan-freaking-tastic! Why me?

I burst onto the next level and briefly worried that I'd chosen the wrong direction, but then I heard the door shatter below, and who fucking cared if I went the wrong way, as long as it was away?

I swore under my breath and took off running down the new hallway, pushing my trembling body harder. Another crash echoed behind me, and my heart slammed against my ribs.

Why had I summoned the Devil? Why hadn't I

read the fine print? Why had I thought I could outsmart the asshole? So fucking stupid.

"Heya, new girl!" a bubbly voice chirped at my side.

I gaped at the petite horned woman suddenly running beside me, all smiles and cheer. Was she nuts?!

"Name's Mara!" She held out her hand. "Lucifer's favourite demon guard."

I shot her an incredulous look. "Are you insane? We're about to become demon chow, and you're introducing yourself?"

Mara laughed, her carefree demeanour irritating given my circumstances. "Oh, I've seen worse. Besides, it's not every day Lucifer drags a living, breathing mortal down here. You must be excited!"

I snorted. "Excited? More like terrified. And you're not helping."

Mara skipped alongside me, unfazed by the chaos behind us.

She blinked obliviously as I thumbed back at our pursuers.

"Little *help* maybe?!"

Her laughter echoed. "But you're doing so well on your own!"

A dead end appeared out of nowhere. I skidded to

a halt, my heart doing a wild drum solo against my ribcage as I faced my not-so-pleasant fate.

Turning back, I got a full view of the demons. They were like a walking, snarling horror show. Humanoid, sure, but twisted and wrong, like someone had tried to assemble them without instructions. Their skin was a sickly shade of... I don't know, some colour that shouldn't exist. And their eyes... oh my goddess, that was the worst part — glowing like those creepy night-lights you see in horror flicks. It was like staring into a nightmare's soul. And the hunger in them – it was like they hadn't eaten in years, and I was the first all-you-can-eat buffet they'd stumbled upon.

CHAPTER SIX

BRONWYN

"*A*h, good. We're here."

She knocked on a solid stone wall beside us, and, to my surprise, a door opened.

Her laughter surrounded me before her clawed fingers wrapped around my wrist and she yanked me through the doorway.

My breath escaped in a hysterical laugh. Saved by a demon in Hell itself. How perfectly absurd. Or at least, I assumed she was a demon. She looked normal, minus the horns.

The door slammed shut behind us, plunging us into

complete and endless darkness. The demons shrieked their fury on the other side of the stone.

What fresh madness was *this*?!

The darkness pressed in around us, and I couldn't see my hand in front of my face.

"Well! That was invigorating."

"Invigorating?!" I snorted, my heart still crashing inside my ribs. "We're trapped inside a wall while the demon mutts—"

"Demon *Legion*," she corrected, her tone perfectly calm, like this was a regular stroll. "No relation to yours truly of course."

Of course?

"Demon *whatevers* are scratching outside, hungering for my bones! What exactly is the plan here, starve to death while we wait for them to give up?" I asked, my voice laced with sarcasm. It helped keep the panic at bay, or at least that's what I told myself.

The muffled sounds of the demons on the other side of the stone wall filled the air—scratching, howling, and all sorts of ungodly noises.

She giggled. "So delightfully dramatic! You'll fit right in. But no no, they won't give up. They've got eternity, you know. Patience is like… their thing. Fortunately, it's too much effort for them to wriggle through stone." Claws clicked on bricks behind me. "Mostly," she muttered in an ominous tone before returning to her regular cheerful programming. "But no matter! While we wait, why not continue the tour?"

"You're joking, right? We're in a wall. A wall. And we're on the menu for demonic fiends."

She laughed again, her voice bouncing off the enclosed space. "Darling, nothing says you can't enjoy the scenery before you die. Come on, trust me. I know some great spots."

Was she high?

Resigned to the absurdity of my situation, I sighed. "Fine. Show me the wonders of Hell."

I shuffled after her chattering, moving deeper into the narrow passage. We hadn't taken more than five steps before I bumped into her with a surprised grunt.

"Oh, apologies!" Mara's voice tinkled with amusement. A small orb of light appeared, casting a dim glow around us. "Better?"

I blinked, my eyes taking a moment to adjust to the light after the darkness.

"This is the Infernal Throne," she said, her voice echoing off the walls. "The seat of Lucifer's power, a formidable fortress no one dares threaten."

I squinted in the dim light. "Looks more like a creepy underground bunker to me."

"You're in a hidden passageway, silly. The rest of

the citadel looks nothing like this." Mara's voice was laced with pride. "Lucifer didn't want a palace. He wanted power, strength... something unbreakable."

I raised an eyebrow. "That's one way to overcompensate."

Mara laughed, a sound that was too merry for this infernal place. "I like you." Then she sobered. "But the Infernal Throne is a marvel. Built from the bones of ancient demons, it's the heart of Hell's power structure and it gets better." She clapped her hands in excitement, giving me whiplash with her shifting emotions. "Lucifer didn't just throw a bunch of bones together. Each one was chosen for its power and history. It's like... Hell's version of an antique collection."

Was she serious? A throne of bones sounded like something out of a horror film.

"Lucifer's tastes are... unique. He chose a citadel over a palace because he values strength over opulence. This place," her voice grew soft, almost reverent, "is a testament to his strength, a fortress against any who would dare challenge him."

I rolled my eyes. "Because nothing screams 'strength' like living in a glorified boneyard." The absurdity of it all was starting to wear thin. I was in Hell, talking architecture with a demon.

"Exactly! You're getting it." Mara clapped her

hands, the sound echoing weirdly. "And let me tell you, the gossip here? Better than any soap opera. Did you know Lucifer once threw a feast for the most malevolent souls, just to prove a point to Beelzebub?"

"Can't say that's come up in conversation lately," I deadpanned.

"Oh, it was a spectacle!" Mara gushed. "Imagine the most twisted souls, all trying to outdo each other. And Lucifer sat there, watching it unfold."

Mara giggled, the sound incongruent with the setting. "But that's nothing compared to the time when—"

I cut her off, my patience thinning. "Look, as riveting as Hell's version of reality TV is, shouldn't we be focusing on getting out of here? Unless you plan on making me a permanent resident?"

Her laughter faded, replaced by a more severe tone. "Escape? Darling, no one escapes Hell. But don't worry, I'll keep you entertained. After all, what's a little eternal damnation among friends?"

Friends? The word tasted like ash in my mouth. I was stuck in a nightmare, and my only ally appeared to be a demon with a penchant for dramatics.

I couldn't stay here. If Lucifer caught up with me, it would be the end. I had to get back to the mortal realm and complete the spell to bring my grandmother back.

Except some small, niggling voice pointed out that he'd find me with ease.

"… collecting rare, enchanted mirrors. They say he spends hours gazing at his reflection, pouting about not having the charm…"

Assuming I could get out, there had to be a way to hide from him. Why hadn't I grabbed the grimoire before he'd transported us to Hell? It would be just my luck if the answers were in that book and I'd left it behind.

"… a feast made entirely of mythical beasts. The chefs are running around trying to find a phoenix. A *phoenix*! As if those are just lying around."

I frowned at the back of her head. Why would anyone want to eat a phoenix?

I shook my head. I needed to focus on myself, not the potential destruction of a rare and precious creature. Lucifer's castle was supposedly impenetrable. If I wanted to escape, I needed to find a weakness, a vulnerability in this place. Something that would lead me to freedom.

There's nothing waiting for you. Why are you so desperate to escape?

True, but there was nothing for me down here either. Lucifer would kill me as soon as he found me and if he didn't, what would my existence be? Nine months attached to a brooding asshole prone to life-threatening temper tantrums? No, thanks.

"Oh, and you should have seen the Miss Hell competition last year! The drama, the backstabbing, the outfits! It was to die for!" She shot me a vicious yet gleeful grin over her shoulder. "Lilith tried to rig the whole thing in favour of her succubus protegée, and Belial challenged her to a duel—"

"Wait!" I stopped in my tracks. "Are you telling me that Hell has beauty pageants?"

She stared at me. "Where do you think the human realm got the concept?" She shook her head, tutting to herself as she started moving again. "Hell has it all. Beauty pageants, gladiator tournaments, cooking competitions, you name it. You'd be amazed at the lengths demons go to for a little entertainment."

"Let me guess, the prize for Miss Hell is a lifetime supply of fire and brimstone?"

She giggled, her clawed fingers tapping against the walls as we walked. "No, no. The winner gets a day as Lucifer's personal assistant. A coveted position, I assure you."

I snorted. "That sounds more like a punishment than a prize."

"Depends on your perspective, I suppose." She

shrugged. "Some demons would kill for the chance to be close to the Devil."

What would I have to do to convince Lucifer to take one of them as his baby mama instead of me?

Eventually, Mara halted. "Here we are!" She spun to face me, eyes glinting in the dim light.

I shot her a sceptical look. "More doors in walls, I presume?"

She rapped the stones, and of course, another doorway opened. Blinding light filtered in, making me wince.

We emerged smack into a huge glowing chamber crammed with towering shelves. Despite my need to get out of hell as fast as possible, my jaw dropped in awe.

She smiled brightly. "Welcome to the Archives of Anguish! Containing every tormented soul's records." Her smile turned shark-like. "Lucifer does so love his paperwork."

I tore my gaze from mountains of crumbling scrolls. "Seriously? Even in the afterlife, there's bureaucracy?"

"Hell has a system, darling. Souls need to be properly catalogued. Can't have one slipping through the cracks and escaping."

Trying not to imagine what anguish records entailed, I asked, "So Hell's just, what, a giant evil library crossed with the world's worst museum?"

Mara tilted her head, blinking slowly as she considered my words. "An apt analogy. The true treasure is suffering, recorded for posterity! But most come simply to... indulge certain proclivities."

A high-pitched scream in the distance had me jolting. She gently took my arm, steering us from the halls of endless agony ledgers. "Perhaps we should move this along…"

CHAPTER SEVEN

BRONWYN

Mara waved me toward the hallway, moving through ornate halls and pointing out sights from wide arched windows.

"The Eternal Pyres," she said, pointing to pyres flickering ominously in a vast courtyard below, "Where the damned burn for all eternity, and the fires never wane. Quite romantic, if you're into that kind of thing."

I glanced out and raised an eyebrow. "Romantic? Seriously?"

"Sure! Nothing says love like eternal flames." She glanced down at the patches of flames, pursing her lips.

"It's one of the old school infernal courting steps. Nobody does it any more."

My brows shot up. "Then why are they still burning?"

"Some people like the drama." She shrugged, then chuckled darkly and turned her back on the pyres. "A few years ago, this greed demon got it in his head that we'd be perfect together. He was that type."

She glanced back over her shoulder at the window, her eyes glazing over.

"The masochistic type?"

"What?" She startled, her gaze meeting mine in confusion for a second. "Oh! No, no. The romantic, 'I'll prove my love by burning in the pits of hell for you' type." Her lips twisted. "Didn't matter how many times I told him I wasn't interested. I wonder what happened to him."

"I think I have a pretty good idea," I muttered, my voice weak as I stared down at the pyres.

Why would anyone do that for someone? Whether they loved them or not.

"Does it hurt?" I asked, unable to tear my eyes away.

"Hmm, of course." She said it like I'd lost my mind. "Where would the fun be if it didn't? They can't die, if that's what you're really asking. It takes more than some fire to kill a denizen of hell."

Black figures writhed in the air around the flaming pillars, their movements swirling and carving out symbols in the sky. My eyes narrowed on them, trying to decipher the weird partners. It almost looked like a message of some kind.

"Those are the Burning Scriptures," she noted, "used to fuel the fires with the best heresies."

I... didn't know what to do with that.

Would all of this become normal to me if I stayed in Hell too long?

Goddess, I hoped not.

Mara pranced ahead, oblivious to my inner turmoil. "Beautiful, isn't it?" she called back over her shoulder.

"What's is?"

"Hell, silly." She spun on the spot, walking backwards and grinning at me. "Lucifer designed Hell not just as a realm of punishment, but as a reflection of his mind. Intricate, complex, and oh-so-meticulous."

"Sounds like a control freak."

She laughed. "Oh, he is. Every stone, every flame, it's all a part of his grand design."

We turned a corner, and a massive, intricately carved hall appeared, filled with statues. They were...

well, bizarre was an understatement. Some looked almost human, frozen mid-motion, like dancers caught in a snapshot. Others were creepy, with limbs twisted in impossible angles, half-human, half-something else. A shapeshifter caught mid-transformation, maybe?

I followed Mara to the centre of the room, weaving between the shapes, eying them with caution like they might start moving if I blinked at the wrong moment.

She stopped in front of one in particular, staring up at it with dreamy eyes. One side of his face was total eye-candy. But the other half? Nightmare central, with a mouth that could probably bite a car in half. And those eyes— oh boy, one looked like it was about to cry, and the other was all *I'm gonna eat your soul*.

She sighed. "This is my favourite."

Of course, it was.

It could have been worse, I guessed. She could have stopped in front of the lady-snake, a woman who looked like she was either trying to charm you or run away from her snake bottom half.

They were all like something out of a horror artist's fever dream. Their expressions were a mix of agony and ecstasy, making me wonder if they were in pain or enjoying it.

"What in the Goddess's name is this place?"

"The Hall of Frozen Souls," Mara said, flinging out

her arms, as if presenting a masterpiece. "Lucifer's personal art gallery. He believes there's beauty in suffering."

"I think he and I have very different definitions of beauty," I muttered. "So, this place, Hell... it's all about fear and pain?"

"Not entirely." Her tone shifted to something more reflective as she stared up at the statue. "Lucifer's Hell is about balance. Fear and pain, yes, for those who deserve it. The rest of us live our lives in relative peace and safety. We prefer things a little…" she waved her hands, searching for the right words. "Spicy. But power and order are also important. He's big on order."

I followed Mara out of the macabre gallery, chewing on her words.

None of it made sense.

Lucifer fixating on order seemed like a bad joke. If order meant that much to him, why make a deal that would seal our fates together for nine months, only to try and kill me before the deal was fulfilled?

"…and that's why the lower dungeons are arranged in a precise hexagonal pattern, each cell exactly the same size. Lucifer believes in equal punishment for all." Mara kept up an endless stream of chatter, her voice a light, tinkling stream in the heavy air of Hell.

Whether she noticed that I wasn't listening, I

couldn't say. I followed her and let my thoughts consume me.

Why the wild mood swings? The last thing he exuded was balance. The man was more like one of those terrifying see-saws I played on as a kid. Or like trying to piece together a puzzle with half the pieces missing — or maybe the pieces were from different boxes.

Really, the answer was easy. "He's a psychotic asshole," I scoffed under my breath.

Mara glanced back at me, her eyes curious. "You don't believe me?"

I shrugged, a half-hearted attempt at nonchalance. "It's not that I don't believe you. It's…" I hesitated, searching for the right words. "My experience with him has been less 'orderly' and more 'don't believe a word I say because I'm going to skewer you with a sword.'"

"Well, of course. His whole modus operandi is to be unpredictable." She laughed as if I should have known something so logical. "His enemies can't best him if they can't pin him down. It's his passion, his fire. Deep down, he craves structure, control. Everything in its right place, including his plans for you."

I bit my lip against my immediate denial that he had plans beyond slitting my throat.

His actions, his anger, all seemed at odds with this

image of a ruler who valued order. Maybe it was all a facade, a mask to hide the chaos underneath. Or maybe, just maybe, there was more to him than met the eye.

We continued our weird tour of the citadel and I tried to silence the never-ending questions about The Devil and his intentions. All I needed to care about was getting out. Why he woke up and chose violence this morning didn't matter.

We stopped at yet another window, and Mara pointed out at what looked like multiple red football fields at the base of the mountain. I had to squint to make it out.

Forget football. Try blood-choked battlefields.

I shuddered. What I assumed were bodies blurred together under a deep violet sky, nothing more than black specks at this distance.

"The Pit of Despair," she said, her tone unaffected by the harrowing sight. "Great for soul-searching, or, well, wallowing."

"Wallowing in despair. Sounds like a real party."

Mara nodded. "Exactly! You're catching on."

We passed more cavernous pits of woe, each creatively dubbed something-or-other Abyss. She rattled them off like tourist attractions: The Abyss of

Massacre, The Blasphemous Abyss, The Abyss of Delusion, The Frozen Abyss.

By the billionth Abyss variation, I snorted. "Okay, is this a joke? Who labelled Hell's pit stops, an emo teenager?"

She blinked innocently. "Lucifer named each one himself."

I rolled my eyes. "Should've guessed. Only Lord Broodiness would turn an architectural feature into a personality trait."

Mara turned to me, her brow furrowed in confusion. "It's no joking matter. Naming holds power here. It's a reflection of the realm's essence."

We descended echoing stairs, approaching a bone-strewn pit where wispy shapes writhed. Lovely. "Let me guess... the Abyss of Extra Abyss-ness?"

"The Abyss of Sorrow actually."

I sighed as we moved on. "So much angst for one postcode…"

We continued down shadowy corridors that felt like they were closing in on us — or maybe that was just me. Mara halted abruptly at one nondescript door. She threw it open, blasting us with scorching air, revealing a yawning, swirling vortex, filled with millions of wailing souls.

"This is The Nexus of Souls."

Each soul within it shimmered like a star in the night sky, weaving an intricate tapestry of light and shadow. The swirling colours — blues, purples, and ghostly whites — danced together in a haunting ballet of lost dreams and whispered secrets.

"Beautiful, isn't it?" she said, but I could hear the edge in her voice.

Beautiful and terrifying — kind of like someone else I knew.

It was mesmerising, like watching the aurora borealis, only a million times more intense. The souls twisted and turned, forming almost deliberate patterns, like they were trying to tell their stories.

I took a step forward, oddly fascinated. The pull was almost physical, the stories of those souls calling to me. It was so pretty.

"Are you insane?" She slapped her hand across my chest, stopping me. "Messy way to expire, being shredded to spiritual essence."

"Noted." I shuddered at the near miss.

She closed the Nexus door with an ominous thud. "If you were mad, it would be fitting for Hell. We're all a bit insane here."

I let out an incredulous laugh. "If you guys set the bar for insanity, I think I'm still several sandwiches short of a picnic."

Mara simply smiled and gestured for me to follow her upstairs. She led me out onto a balcony.

"If you look down, you'll see the Infernal Arena," she said, her voice taking on a note of pride.

I risked peeking over the precipice and immediately wished I hadn't. For my effort, I got a dizzying view of a gladiator-style stadium far below, ringed by jagged obsidian. Even from here, the space reverberated with anguished cries and shrieks of pain. A crimson glow illuminated muscular beasts tearing at broken bodies while cheering shadows packed towering stands. My gut twisted at the sight of it.

I shuddered. "What demented circus is that?"

"The Infernal Games," she explained. "Where demons prove their mettle in battle for the favour of their Dark Lord. The survivors join Lucifer's elite guard."

"And entertainment, I guess," I muttered, recoiling from screaming spectators in the stands.

"Of course." She nodded, her voice matter-of-fact. "If you'd like, I'm sure I could convince Lucifer to let you attend. He has a box, so you'd be quite comfortable."

"Attend? Hard pass. That's barbaric, even for here." I backed firmly away from the edge.

Mara smirked knowingly with a noncommittal

hum, continuing the tour. But the grisly scenes from that arena already haunted me. It was a job to say which of Hell's sights would give me more nightmares. It made me dread to learn what other 'delights' Hell would try to force me to stomach.

I have to get out of here.

We walked on through a series of caverns and halls, each more disturbing than the last. The further we went, the more I despaired of ever finding a way out of this place. At least not without some help.

"Mara… is there a way to get out of hell? Back to my world, realm, plane…" I struggled with the terminology.

She hesitated, her expression turning thoughtful. "There's no easy way if that's what you're asking. Once, there was a stairway connecting all the realms, but it hasn't been used in aeons. It likely crumbled when the balance shifted between the realms."

"A stairway?"

She shrugged, her gaze distant. "It's ancient lore, Bronwyn. The details are lost to time, much like the stairway itself. All I know is that no one has used it for countless centuries."

It sounded like a fairy tale, a myth woven into the fabric of Hell's twisted reality. Probably just another mind game in the Devil's playground... dangling hope in front of me, only to make it impossible to find.

"But you know some of the details?"

She sighed, but indulged me. "It was a connection between all realms, a bridge spanning the fabric of existence. As for where it leads, that depends on the realm it connected to. Your world, another plane, a different realm altogether. No one truly knows."

So if it existed, and if I could find it, it might not take me home. Great.

The shadows swirled in a dark alcove as we passed. There was something hypnotic about it, like those optical illusion paintings where if you stared long enough, you'd see a dolphin or whatever.

As we drew closer, I leaned in, curiosity winning over common sense.

Big mistake. Huge.

Mara yanked me back so hard I nearly lost my footing. A skeletal hand, all bones and sharp, nasty-looking razor claws, burst from the shadows, swiping at the air where my face had been seconds ago. My heart did a triple somersault, and I'm pretty sure it landed backwards.

CHAPTER EIGHT

BRONWYN

I yelped, stumbling away from the alcove as the skeletal hand scraped the air hungrily before sinking back into the shadows. My heart was pounding like a drum solo at a rock concert. "Holy hellfire, what was that?"

"Despair Shadows," Mara explained, her tone nonchalant as if skeletal hands in the walls were just another Tuesday for her. She smirked at my incredulous look. "They'll gladly feed off you if you wander carelessly. As will the Echoes of Sorrow. Maybe don't go strolling around the Infernal Throne alone, yes?"

I shuddered, skin crawling at the near miss. Lovely — soul-sucking ghouls roaming Hell's halls as if it were some sort of demonic petting zoo. What next?

"Just what I needed, more creepy crawlies in my life."

She chuckled, her eyes dancing with amusement. "My, my, aren't you a resilient one? Not many mortals make it this far without losing their sanity. Lucky you."

"Lucky," I muttered, more to myself than to her. This place was like a twisted amusement park, and I was an unwilling participant strapped into the world's worst roller coaster. I couldn't help but wonder if Lucifer was somewhere laughing at my plight.

As we walked along the outer parapets, Mara gestured down the mountainside with a flourish of her hand. "There's the Circle of Lust. Lilith's domain. This might be a good time for me to warn you about some of the prominent citizens of Hell. It's good to know who to avoid, you see." She spoke like a tour guide in the world's most macabre museum.

I raised a brow, my curiosity piqued despite the anxiety gnawing at me like a starved rat. "I thought everyone here was a potential threat."

She nodded sagely, her expression serious. "True, but some are more dangerous than others. Take Lilith, for example. The Lord of Lust. She's got an agenda, and she's always looking for new playthings. Cross her path, and she might find you too intriguing a snack to pass up." Her words sent a chill down my spine.

Far below, Lilith's domain sprawled out, the land covered in a hazy crimson atmosphere that pulsed with its own sinister life. Cries and groans, the chorus of the damned, echoed up from somewhere within that scarlet fog.

I shuddered, imagining what infernal creatures the immortal seductress kept for company in her circle of sin.

"My hands are full with the drama king Devil, thanks," I scoffed, my voice a mix of disbelief and a poorly masked tremor of fear.

As we peered over the edge, gazing into the smoking abyss of broiling lava flows, Mara outlined various demon lords who ruled the circles, each of whom might take an... unnatural interest, given my still-breathing state.

She smirked, her eyes glinting with a dark mirth. "Beelzebub is the gluttonous lord. Always scheming, always hungry. You want to keep your distance unless you want to be part of some elaborate feast."

"No thanks. I prefer not to be on the menu." I tried

to inject a bit of humour into my voice, but it came out more strangled than I intended.

"Smart choice." She pointed to another area of the lava-scarred landscape, where an ominous greenish hue oozed from the ground. "And there's Envy, Abaddon's Circle. Watch your back around him. He'll use any opportunity to get ahead."

I sighed, feeling the weight of the information settling on my shoulders. "So, basically, Hell is full of backstabbers and power-hungry demons. Got it."

"You're getting it," she said with a wink. "But you, my dear, are a wildcard. No one really knows what to make of you. If they know you're here at all."

Hopefully, that was true and I just had to stay out of the crosshairs of their attention until I found a way out.

As we left the dungeons behind, the air grew colder, and the scent of decay lingered like the world's worst perfume. I hesitated, brushing my fingertips against a dark wall, curiosity my absolute worst trait.

White-hot agony speared through my mind, and I recoiled as if I'd been electrocuted. I cried out, images flashing behind my eyes as I collapsed.

My mother dropping me at my grandmother's house when I was thirteen, shrieking and crying but still abandoning me...

The scene shifted.

I was back in my grandmother's warm, cosy kitchen. Rowena's gentle hands were guiding mine as we stirred a cauldron, her laughter a soothing balm. "Bronwyn, my dear," she said, her voice rich with affection, "You have such a bright spirit. Don't ever let the world dim it."

Her face, lined with the wisdom of years and the kindness of a thousand smiles, filled my view, making me smile.

Then the memory twisted.

Her lifeless form on the deathbed, her once vibrant eyes closed forever, leaving me adrift in a world suddenly too large and too cold.

Mara tutted. "I did say to watch your step. The walls here have a mind of their own." Her voice was a distant echo, barely penetrating the storm of pain and memories raging in my head.

I rubbed my temples, trying to shake off the residual agony. "What's happening to me?" I gasped, my voice weak and trembling.

"An Echo has you, I'm afraid. Nasty tricksters," she said, her tone unexpectedly serious, a stark contrast to her usual playful demeanour.

I clutched my head, the coven's rejection, the sting

of their words, and the crushing loneliness that followed replayed in my mind. "How do I stop it?"

"You don't." Her tone was firm, brooking no argument. "Try to relax. I'll have you loose in a jiffy."

Tears spilled down my cheeks.

Images flickered behind my eyelids, unbidden and cruel. I saw myself, younger and more naive, clutching a teddy bear with one eye missing, waiting for hours by the window for a dad who never showed. The sting of abandonment was as sharp as a knife, slicing through years of buried emotions.

The echo morphed into the laughter of schoolkids, taunting me for my oddness, my affinity for the shadows and the whispers of unseen things. I remembered shrinking into myself, wishing I could disappear.

And then, there was him — my first love, his face now blurred by time. The warmth of his hand in mine, the promise of forever in his eyes — all shattered in a moment.

"There's something not right about you."

Each memory was a thread in the tapestry of my life, woven with pain and loss. I gasped, a sob escaping my lips as the weight of years of loneliness and misunderstanding pressed down on me.

I was the outcast, the misfit, the one who never belonged anywhere.

I closed my eyes tighter, trying to block out the images, the grief threatening to consume me like a ravenous beast.

After what felt like an eternity, the visions released their clawing grip. I panted, glaring at the dark space as if it were a living entity that had attacked me.

Was it living?

Though what did it matter in the scheme of things?

Mara patted my shoulder. "Their weapon is grief. Best not to let them snare you to begin with."

I gasped, the weight lifting from my chest. The memories faded, and I found myself standing in the dimly lit corridor, shaken, coated in sweat, but free.

Heart pounding, I grabbed Mara's wrist in desperation. "I can't stay here another minute... please, you have to show me a way out of here!" The words tumbled out, a torrent of fear and determination.

She blinked, her expression unreadable. "I understand this is difficult, but you just got here. Maybe it won't look so bad in a year?"

"A year!" I screeched, the absurdity of her suggestion almost laughable if it weren't so horrifying."The Diva Devil will have murdered me by then."

"I'm sure that's not true, and besides, sometimes, the only way out is through. Facing what's in front of you instead of seeking escape."

"That's easy for you to say," I snapped, my patience wearing thin. "You live here. I don't belong in this nightmare world."

Mara's gaze softened, and for a moment, I glimpsed a flicker of sympathy. "Hell is what you make of it. It can break you or mould you. But seeking escape might lead you to a fate far worse."

Her words died as we rounded the corner and I slammed directly into a voluptuous figure. I stumbled back, stunned to find myself staring into hypnotic emerald eyes.

"Oh, dear," Mara muttered under her breath, her voice a mixture of resignation and wariness.

"Well well... you must be Lucifer's new pet." Her voice was like velvet, smooth and seductive. She trailed a long-nailed finger down my cheek, and I shuddered as wicked delight sparked in her stare. "We're going to have such fun, you and I…"

Absolutely fucking not.

I stumbled backwards, my heart racing, almost tripping over my own feet.

Mara cleared her throat, her voice cutting through the thick air. "A pleasure as always, Lilith. Sadly, we must be going."

"So soon?" Lilith tutted, her voice laced with feigned disappointment as she followed my retreat with an enticing sway of her hips. Her long nails trailed lazily along the wall, unconcerned that a shadow being might ensnare her, a predator playing with her prey. "But we only just met. You don't really have to leave, do you, Bronwyn?"

CHAPTER NINE

LUCIFER

*T*hirty minutes earlier…

I walked into the assembly room, a grand chamber ensconced in undulating shadows, each corner whispering secrets of bygone eras. The air was thick with the scent of ancient power, a heady blend of smouldering embers and time-worn leather, tinged with a faint, almost imperceptible trace of brimstone.

The Lords of Sin, each a paragon of their respective vice, gathered around the obsidian table, their eyes ablaze with infernal hunger even while they exuded an air of indifference.

I took my rightful place at the head of the council,

my gaze sweeping across them with a mixture of disdain and weary resignation.

Beelzebub sprawled lazily in his chair, his rotund figure draped in rich, albeit soiled, garments, his eyes glinting with insatiable hunger. He gnawed on a bone, his lips smeared with the remnants of a feast only he could appreciate.

Beside him, Belphegor lounged, eyes glazed with disinterest; he barely registered my presence. His posture was one of utter disengagement, a being so consumed by ennui that the weight of his head was too much to bear.

Moloch, Lord of Wrath, sat rigidly, his hands clenched into fists. His eyes, burning with a perpetual fire, flickered with barely contained rage. The air around him crackled.

Abbadon, representing envy, was a study in contrasts. His eyes, a piercing green, bore into mine with an unsettling intensity. He shifted uncomfortably, his form shimmering as if unable to settle into a single shape.

Mammon, the embodiment of greed, sat meticulously counting his coins, his attention fixated on his hoard. His fingers, thin and grasping, clinked the gold with obsessive precision, his gaze never straying from his precious treasure.

Belial, the epitome of pride, sat with an air of superiority that made my own seem modest. His chin was lifted, his eyes half-lidded in a perpetual state of condescension. Every inch of him exuded a sense of grandeur and self-importance that was almost palpable.

And lastly, Lilith. She watched me with an intensity that belied her seductive poise. The Lord of Lust, her gaze was a cauldron of desire and cunning. Dressed in a gown that clung to her like a second skin, she exuded an allure that was both perilous and intoxicating.

As I observed them, a mix of contempt and amusement churned within me. These beings, once fearsome in their power, now seemed almost caricatures of themselves, so deeply entrenched in their sins.

And yet, they were mine to command, a motley crew bound to my will, for better or worse.

With a sigh, I addressed them, my voice resonating with a regal authority that echoed through the vast chamber: "No doubt, rumours are circulating regarding my recent guest." A stir rippled through the room. "You'll be pleased to know that our pact with The Morrigan is moving forward. Soon I, and Hell itself, shall draw more power from the core, restoring our realm to its once glorious state."

A subtle murmur of approval rumbled around the

room, like serpents hissing in the dark. They leaned forward, their eyes gleaming with delight.

"The Owen witch is bound by an infernal contract. She is mine for the next nine months. During this time, she is to be protected at all costs." I directed a hard look at Lilith before looking each of the other Lords dead in the eyes. "Should I learn you have defied me, there will be consequences."

Murmurs of acquiescence rippled around the table. Lilith only smirked. None would openly defy my claim, whatever they privately pondered regarding this strange affair.

"We are pleased with your progress, Lucifer," said Mammon. "The Circle of Greed will pledge our allegiance to your heir, as we did you."

I inclined my head, silently thanking the demon.

"Lucifer, a father." Abbadon chuckled. "Who would have thought the day would actually come?"

"Indeed, the prospect is thrilling." I was anything but thrilled.

Yes, the power boost would be welcome, but for what cost? My eternity tied to a witch who would give anything to escape Hell?

A desperate witch was a dangerous witch, and thanks to The Morrigan, I couldn't kill her.

If these demons knew The Morrigan had shackled

me to a witch who was stupid enough to summon the Devil, they'd laugh about it for millennia. It would degrade their trust in my strength and make them question whether the new world order should include new leadership.

I couldn't let that happen.

Which meant getting Bronwyn under control and fast. If we worked together…

The pleasantries and congratulations echoed around the table, but my mind was firmly entrenched in solving my predicament. Or at least finding a path that benefited myself and my domain.

The prospect of fatherhood didn't thrill me; it bound me to a fate I never desired.

Keeping Bronwyn in Hell would remove a piece of that issue. It would ensure that the child had its mother nearby, providing stability in what would surely be a dangerous upbringing.

But that would mean an Owen witch, with her mortal concepts and rebellious spirit, influencing the heir to my dominion.

No, that would not do.

Which meant somehow sending the witch home eventually, and the only way to do that would require breaking the bond.

There had to be a way.

Under normal circumstances, the female would be able to reject the bonds, but I had spent countless hours now studying the threads binding us. There were no chinks in its flawless design, as there should have been. The Morrigan had no intention of allowing us to reject her 'gift.'

"That's all for today," I said, standing so that they would take the hint to move quickly. "We shall reconvene next week."

Their conversations lingered, my words lost in their discussions about realms and alliances. I maintained my outward composure. Patience was a virtue, even in hell.

Not that it truly mattered with how distracted I was. There had to be an easy way to persuade the witch to support me. She was still desperate to get her grandmother back. Perhaps I could offer to find her in exchange for her unwavering, unquestioning participation in destroying the bond?

It would be painful. I couldn't convince myself of any other reality. So having some tangible leverage that would force her compliance in seeing the task through to the end might be for the best.

Movement caught my eye. Lilith.

She slipped quietly out the door, but not before I caught a glimpse of her devious smirk. That woman had meddling on the mind.

Mere moments later, a spike of fear surged through the soulbond with the witch.

What was that infernal woman doing now?

The soulbond thrummed with elevating distress as I stalked the Infernal Throne halls. Turning a corner, I froze, ice flooding my veins at the scene before me.

Lilith had Bronwyn pinned to the stones, claw-tipped fingers trailing suggestively down her throat. My witch looked near panic, her face white, and her eyes wider than I'd ever seen. Not even facing my sword did she look so terrified.

"Come play in my circle, little one," Lilith all but purred. "I can teach you wonders beyond his simple realm…"

"Lilith!" Power filled my voice. It swept into the hallway and wrapped itself around the demoness. "What part of *the witch is under my protection* did you not understand?"

"Lucifer." Lilith shuddered at the feel of my power gripping her. Her eyes fluttered shut and a sinister yet delighted smile curved her lips. "I wondered when you'd join us. We were getting to know each other, weren't we, Bronwyn?"

Bronwyn's eyes flashed with defiance, but the tension in her frame betrayed her discomfort. As much as I resented her for her part in my current predicament, I couldn't in good conscience leave her to fend for herself. I'd only lasted ten minutes before I'd sent Mara, my best guard, to trail her earlier today.

I regarded Lilith with a cold gaze, my composure unyielding. "Release her. Your games do not amuse me."

Her smirk widened, undeterred by my stern tone. "Oh, but we were just chatting, weren't we, Bronwyn? I'm sure Lucifer wouldn't mind if you took a little stroll outside with me. A breath of fresh air, perhaps?"

Bronwyn's eyes flicked to mine, a silent plea for rescue. Lilith's taunts were laced with a suggestive undercurrent, aiming to coax her into leaving my protection.

"That won't be happening." I stepped between them, forcing Lilith to back away or risk touching me, which would constitute an attack on the King of Hell.

Lilith arched a brow, feigning innocence as she retreated. "Such possessiveness, Lucifer. It's not healthy. Let the little bird spread her wings."

Ignoring her, I extended my hand toward Bronwyn, a silent invitation for her to stand behind me. She hesitated, studying me with shrewd eyes for a moment before ultimately giving in and using me as a shield.

Lilith sighed dramatically. "Spoilsport. Well, if you're going to keep your pet on a leash, I suppose I'll find other amusements."

She sashayed away with a calculated parting glance, and Bronwyn sagged against my back, breathing shallowly. It lasted all of a second before she stiffened and backed away from me.

"What was that about?" the witch asked, suspicion lacing her words. "Another of your minions sent to kill me?"

"No. Lilith enjoys her games, and you, petal, are an unwitting player. Now, I suggest we leave before she decides on another round."

Bronwyn eyed me with suspicion, her wariness etched in the set of her jaw. I tried to dismiss Mara, but Bronwyn baulked.

"So, what? You're just going to send her away so you can have another go at killing me without witnesses? Is that it?"

I chuckled at the accusation, finding her paranoia oddly endearing. "As if lack of witnesses would hinder the Devil."

She crossed her arms, unimpressed by my reassurances. "Forgive me if I'm not entirely convinced of your sudden benevolence. You're still the man — thing — that tried to skewer me with a sword earlier today."

I sighed. "If it eases your fretting…" One nail shifted into a claw.

She yelped and backed away, almost falling into a shadowy corner. Mara caught her, tugging her away before she could meet the resident.

"What did I say about dark corners?" she tutted.

Shaking my head, I sliced a claw across my palm, allowing blood to flow. "By my blood, I vow no harm unto you this day."

The oath shimmered in the air before fading.

"This day?" Bronwyn asked, her tone suggesting she was anything but appeased. "What about tomorrow or a month from now? I'm stuck here for nine months, aren't I?"

With a scowl, I sliced my palm open and repeated the vow with the longer time frame. "Happy?"

Bronwyn's shoulders eased, though she still watched me with caution in her stormy eyes.

Finally, I dismissed Mara and gestured for the witch to follow me. We walked in tense silence. Her gaze bore into me, her thoughts so loud they screamed in my mind. Wincing, I blocked her out before she could give me a headache.

"Aren't you gallant all of a sudden?" Distrust

dripped from her sarcastic words. "What happened to all the murder attempts?"

I smirked, surprisingly enjoying how she challenged me. "Alliances in Hell are ever-shifting, petal. It would be wise for you to adapt."

Her eyes narrowed, clearly not satisfied with my vague response. "Why the sudden need to protect me?"

I sighed, cursing the witch's defining trait: curiosity. "Demon politics. The intricacies are beyond your mortal understanding."

"Try me."

I allowed a sly grin to play on my lips. "Some conversations are better held away from listening ears, and trust me, the walls here have many."

She took a step back, paling as her gaze flitted around the dimly lit corridor. The shadows whispered their secrets, adding an air of sinister mystery to our surroundings.

"The walls have... ears?" she finally sputtered. "What else is this damned place going to throw at me?"

"Damned is right."

Her expression hardened as she fixed me with those eyes that could force an unprepared fallen angel to his knees. "I've had enough surprises for one day," she said, her voice hard yet uncertain. "This place is nothing like

I imagined, but also exactly like I imagined. I need some straightforward answers."

"Straightforward answers are a rare commodity in Hell. But for the sake of easing your mind, let me assure you that our little chat will not involve any unsavoury surprises."

"Meaning you aren't going to try to kill me again?"

"No." I held up my hand. "Trust the oath, Bronwyn."

"That's easy for you to say. You're the Devil. I'm just trying to survive this madness."

"Your definition of 'survival' might need some refinement in this realm," I said as we walked, my tone casual, almost teasing. "It's not about staying alive. It's about thriving despite the chaos."

She shot me a sidelong glance. "Thriving in Hell? What Twilight Zone kind of bullshit is that?"

CHAPTER TEN

*B*ronwyn

"Start talking, brimstone breath. What's your endgame? Why the sudden buddy treatment?"

I eyed the room warily. It was perfect. Not a blood-stain, a smashed piece of furniture or torn tapestry to be found. Maybe Hell had some magical cleanup crew, or Lucifer was really good at hiding his mess. The lack of visible damage didn't ease my discomfort.

What else could he make disappear?

"You'll want to sit for this," he said, gesturing to an ornate chair. I glared at it like it personally insulted me.

I snorted, crossing my arms as I leaned against the opposite wall after inspecting it for shadows. "Think I'll stand, actually." As if I was letting my guard down around Sir Stabsalot so soon! "Explain why you tried to turn me into a kebab."

Lucifer sighed as he dragged a hand through his hair. "It wasn't personal. I thought... Well, I hoped that killing you would break the bond."

I canted my head, my brows puckering in confusion. "What bond?"

He grimaced, like he'd rather be anywhere else than explaining whatever fresh hell he'd dropped me in. And considering the place, that's saying something.

"The Morrigan, she... bound us together. Soulbound, to be precise."

I blinked, the idea taking a moment to register. The word niggled at a distant memory, something I'd read in one of my grandmother's books and shrugged off as absolute nonsense. No one had heard from The Morrigan, goddess of witches, in centuries.

Why would anyone care about her soulbonds if she wasn't around to gift them?

Clearly, I should have paid more attention.

"Soulbound? As in supernatural magical marriage?"

Hopefully, he was messing with me. I mean, if The Morrigan was gone, it had to be a joke.

"Unfortunately, yes." He nodded, his expression

serious. Too serious for my liking. "Eternally linked. Every emotion, every sensation, shared between us."

I stared at his feet, the tapestry, anywhere but him. He couldn't be… it had to be…

"The Morrigan is gone. She can't bond people together if she doesn't exist anymore."

"Oh, she exists," he muttered, his tone dark. "But if you need proof…?"

He started unbuttoning his shirt. The action reminded me of what we did last night, against the wall I now used to prop myself up. I moved to the fireplace, my face burning.

He cleared his throat when I refused to look at him. Nestled right over his heart, weaving through his existing tattoos, lay a circular design unlike anything I'd ever seen. It was intricate, a Celtic knotwork of loops and lines that twined together in an endless dance. It pulsed with an energy that called to me, soothed me.

I resisted the urge to let out a sardonic laugh. "Oh, fantastic. So, my emotional baggage is now the Devil's carry-on."

His lips twitched, acknowledging the absurdity. "In a nutshell, yes."

Would it be so bad? a small voice whispered enticingly in the back of my mind.

Yes. Yes, it would be fucking awful. I didn't need the

details to know that this damned bond had put a snag in my plans to escape Hell.

"This wasn't a violation I foresaw when I entered into our bargain…" He trailed off, not quite meeting my glare.

My eyes widened as the pieces settled into place.

"Is this why you went ginsu knife happy on me earlier?" I gasped. "It was. You were trying to file for magical divorce the ultra messy way. Oh my goddess."

He scratched the back of his head, avoiding my gaze like a kid caught with his hand in the biscuit barrel. "I thought severing you from the equation would sever the bond. Turns out, I was wrong."

A delighted grin claimed my lips as I remembered a slash magically appearing on his body. "Did the Devil get a taste of his own medicine?"

He winced, and for a moment, the mighty Lucifer seemed more like a normal guy who'd screwed up his chances at a second date. "Worse. Any harm I inflict on you bounces back on me threefold."

I snorted. "And you didn't expect that from the goddess of witches?"

Then I laughed some more, tears leaking from the corner of my eyes as I well and truly lost it. Who could blame me after the twenty-four hours I'd had?

"Well, isn't that poetic justice? The Devil, haunted by the consequences of his own misdeeds."

"This bond is not to be taken lightly." His gaze darkened, his tone deadly serious. It sobered me slightly. Slightly. "It's binding. We're stuck with each other for the long haul unless…"

My eyes narrowed on him. If he thought he was going to take another whack at ending me, he had another think coming.

"Unless what?"

The idea of being stuck with the Devil for eternity, sharing feelings and whatnot, wasn't exactly the happily-ever-after I'd imagined. Sure, I'd signed a contract, but this wasn't part of the deal.

"Well, petal," he drawled. "You could always help me find a way to sever the bond."

"Help you?" I scoffed, crossing my arms in defiance. "After you tried to turn me into a human shish kebab? That's a hard pass."

He rolled his eyes, slipping off his jacket as if discussing the weather. He dropped it to the floor where it vanished in a puff of smoke. "I already apologised for trying to kill you, didn't I? It was a miscalculation. It won't happen again."

"A miscalculation?" I repeated, disbelief colouring

my tone. "What about the heir you so desperately wanted? Were you going to destroy me and go trick some other unsuspecting witch into being your broodmare?"

"I wasn't in my right mind this morning."

Cryptic motherfucker. "Do you want to hear about the side effects of the bond, or are we going to keep arguing?"

I paled. "What side effects?"

"The bond, once sealed — which it was, last night," he added with a knowing smile that tried to turn my knees to liquid. He shrugged out of his shirt, baring all of that raw tattooed muscle to my starved hormones. I stiffened my knees and glared at him. "It has an interesting side effect. Witches, especially the female ones, temporarily lose control over their magic."

"Lose control how? For how long?"

"Hard to say…" He at least had the decency to look apologetic.

But it did bugger all to ease the sucker punch his words landed.

My throat tightened, panic gripping me tight. Losing control of my magic wasn't an option, not in this place. Hell was a chaotic mess of supernatural horrors, and the last thing I needed was to be the next one running wild.

I sagged against the mantel, legs gone mushy.

"What do you mean, hard to say?" I snapped, frustration bubbling beneath my words. "You can't drop a bomb like that and waltz away with a 'hard to say.' Make a fucking guess."

"It affects each witch differently," he finally admitted. "It's been centuries since this bond existed, the records are… lacking." His brow furrowed and his eyes glossed over. "I remember that covens used to train their witches on how to handle it. There were control techniques of some kind."

My hands balled into fists at my sides, nails digging into my palms. Fury and raw panic warred inside me. Without magic, I was demon chow!

"It'll be okay." Lucifer took a step towards me and I stopped him with a death stare. "You're safe here. None of the denizens of Hell would dare enter my wing without permission. We have to wait out the lust spell anyway and fortunately, that will help you regain control."

"How exactly will days of sex help me regain control of my magic?"

For once, he looked sheepish. "The bond destabilises your power, and our connection strengthens it."

I blushed as an image of the type of connection he meant floated through my mind. My gaze dropped to his bare chest, memories far too close to the surface. Letting him come inside of me should not have made me feel so powerful.

I shouldn't crave it.

"You want to strengthen the bond you intend to break?"

He took another step forward. "I know it seems illogical, but it's the only way. If memory serves, some witches recovered quickly, some took days. The stronger the witch, the longer it lasted."

He said the last part with a pointed look at me.

"Fix it." My demand came out sharper than I intended, the urgency coating every word. "There has to be a way to reverse this."

Lucifer sighed, a mix of sympathy and frustration in his eyes. "I need you to understand. The bond is ancient magic. It's not a flick of a wand and poof, it's gone. We're talking about rewriting fundamental forces here."

I scowled, my frustration boiling over. "I don't care about the fundamental forces. I care about my magic, my control. I can't be some ticking time bomb of supernatural chaos in this hellhole. There's got to be a way to break it."

He held up pacifying hands. "As much as I would

love to rush this, we can't. It would be dangerous to us both, and I do still need that child, Bronwyn."

"So what? I'm meant to accept that I'll never leave hell until you decide it's time to take a risk that might cost me my life?"

If I can convince myself to leave after giving this monster my child, that is. *What kind of mother could leave an innocent child in hell?* It was something my mother would have done for sure, but I was better than her.

"You exaggerate, petal... it doesn't prevent exiting my domain. You simply may find separation... uncomfortable."

Was there no end to the torture in this bloody place? And why did his cologne suddenly smell so freaking delectable?

Lucifer, ever the picture of composure, raised a brow. "I didn't say it was ideal. I said it was possible. You could leave Hell, but it would hurt."

"Oh, how delightful! So, I pack my bags, stroll through the fiery gates, wave goodbye to this demonic circus, but it might cripple me. Is that what you're saying?" I scoffed, a bitter edge to my words.

He nodded, his gaze fixed on mine. "Potentially, yes. It won't be pleasant. The bond, while not a physical chain, connects us on a deeper level. Separation would be... agonising."

Agonising. That word hung in the air like a curse, and I could almost feel the weight of it settling on my shoulders. Agonising, like everything else in this infernal realm.

"You really know how to sell it," I muttered, arms crossed over my chest. "I suppose I should feel grateful for the option, right?"

His lips curved into a half-smile. "Look at it this way, petal," his hands dropped to his belt. He unbuckled it with deft fingers, while snaring me with those ocean-deep eyes. "At least you have a choice. Not everyone in Hell gets that luxury."

"Oh yes, I'm so grateful you tricked me into signing my life away."

He sighed. "It wasn't meant to be your life. I'm no happier about this than you are."

I harrumphed and crossed my arms, not even remotely appeased.

"There is no sense in continuing this animosity. We're stuck together for now." A charming smile softened his expression. I didn't trust it. "How about a truce while I find a way to free us?"

My brow arched. "What kind of truce?"

He smirked. "I'll refrain from trying to end your mortal existence."

"And?" He'd already proven he couldn't kill me

without causing himself harm. I wasn't worried about that anymore.

"I'll keep you safe, allow no other to attempt to kill you on my orders or any others. You'll be treated like a queen, your every need met."

I didn't have any other choice if I wanted to escape hell with my soul and body intact.

"Fine."

He nodded, a pleased glint in his eyes. Then he conjured an hourglass, the sands trickling down with ominous inevitability. Like time itself conspired against me. His lips pressed together and he sighed. He tugged his belt loose, dropping it on the floor, and I tracked it like some sex-starved fool.

"We have minutes before the next round of the lust spell kicks in."

My cheeks combusted as his meaning hit. And they weren't the only spot going a bit melty, if ya know what I mean.

His trousers hit the floor. I was left staring at the strangest cock I had ever seen, trying to keep the drool inside my mouth.

Had I laid eyes on it last time, I would have questioned how something so girthy would fit inside of me. I wasn't certain I could even wrap my hand around it.

And then what I'd imagined to be ridges, really

were in fact ridges. The velvety skin stretched across multiple raised bumps that covered his entire length. I shivered just remembering what those had done to me, touching every nerve and making my toes curl.

He kept talking but I couldn't hear a thing, my attention too engrossed in figuring out what the purplish bulge above his cock was.

"But there's a silver lining," he said, his voice breaking through the fog.

I snorted, unable to fathom any silver lining in this demonic carnival. "I doubt that but do enlighten me."

He grinned, and it was the kind of grin that made you question your life choices. "We'll be settling your magic and fulfilling the contract simultaneously."

My eyebrows shot up in disbelief. "You find humour in the darkest corners of Hell, don't you? Fulfilling the contract with some demon spawn while trying not to burn the whole place down? What a lovely family picture."

He chuckled, the sound sending a shiver down my spine. "Family pictures in Hell have a certain... charm."

"You really need to get your dictionary checked. I doubt 'charming' is in the vocabulary of this fiery pit."

He took another step forward, and I held my hand out, warding him off as I skirted around the bathtub. "Why don't you stay over there and I'll…"

The hourglass ran empty, and an almost impercep-
tible shift in the air signalled the onset of the lust spell.
A surge of desire tangled with my thoughts, and I shot
Lucifer a glare that could melt steel.

CHAPTER ELEVEN

LUCIFER

*W*ith a clap of my hands, Bronwyn's clothes dissolved into thin air. She continued to skirt around me as if either of us had a choice. If I couldn't fight the spell, what hope did she think she would have?

"Come now, petal, you know this is pointless."

"Speak for yourself."

The spell tightened its grip impatiently, flooding me with need, stealing my sense of control. Desperation coiled within me, spiralling tight, begging for satisfaction and release. I groaned, gripping my cock to ease some of the pressure. Her face flushed and her eyes glazed over, the spell impacting her too.

I moved closer, dodging every piece of furniture she tried to place between us, her scent arousing every cell in my being. There was nowhere for her to hide in my domain.

I snarled in mounting frustration as Bronwyn evaded my grasp again. She knew as well as I that resistance was futile, yet still she sought to delay the inevitable.

Her defiance would be admirable, were it not so inconvenient. The compulsion to claim her battered my senses, clawing through my veins like an addiction.

"Cease these games, witch," I bit out through gritted teeth. "You only prolong both our suffering."

As if to mock me, she whirled away once more, grey eyes flashing. "Get stuffed! I don't care if it's magic — I won't be manhandled!"

A feral sound tore from my throat. In a blink, I had her pinned to the wall, my palms slamming into the brick on either side of her head and stone crumbling beneath my touch. Our bodies brushed, my need surging at the contact.

"You forget yourself." My voice was rough with torment. "I am the master here."

"I didn't choose to be here." She lifted her chin

defiantly. "And even if I had, it doesn't mean I have to make this easy for you."

"For us."

The lust spell didn't care either way. It locked us in our dance, trapped us in desire, nudging her towards me even as she tried to deny me. An angry gleam sparked in her eyes that only made me harder. Even naked, she clung onto obsolete threads of pride.

With both hands, I seized her waist, pulling her against my chest, the heat of her teasing my erection.

Staring into her stormy grey eyes while the heat of her licked at my skin, something inside me fractured. With a muffled oath, I crushed my mouth to hers, claiming her lips in a savage kiss. She gasped, stiffening in shock, before melting against me with a helpless moan.

She clung to me, her fingers digging painfully into my arms. But I couldn't feel even a flicker of pain. The feel and taste of her doused my senses. I deepened the kiss ruthlessly. The infernal spell demanded satisfaction and I was helpless but to obey.

She arched into the kiss, her fight dissolving to match my own desire.

Or so I believed. No sooner had I deepened our embrace than Bronwyn bit my lip hard enough to draw blood. She leaned back, eyes blazing while I pressed a finger to the bite.

"Don't think this means you've won," she hissed.

For a second, I couldn't make sense of her words, too fixated on the fact my perfectly mortal witch had sunk her teeth into a divine being. She had no idea what that meant.

The Morrigan mated human witches through her soulbond, but demons and angels used a mating bite. The effects were just as permanent as the soulbond and even knowing that, I grinned, a perverse delight scorching my insides. If she wanted to play on a divine level, all she had to do was ask.

You don't want that. It's just the spell talking.

Ignoring the voice, I chuckled. "Your pride is adorable, petal, but wasted here."

To prove my point, I captured her mouth again. My teeth grazed her lips, taking care not to break the skin. Yet. My tongue delved past her lips to caress her own. She shuddered, helpless sounds escaping her throat even as her fists pounded my chest in protest.

I relished her defiance, the fire that refused to bend entirely to the spell's will. It only heightened my craving for her... Her nails raked down my back, sparking sharp pleasure-pain. "I won't...give in…" she gasped between fevered kisses.

My fingers tangled in her silken hair, holding her in place. "You will," I promised. "I am only beginning to unravel you, my captivating witch."

With a thought, I shifted us across the room, throwing her down on the bed. She gasped as her body settled on the duvet, then she glared up at me.

"Don't do that without warning me!"

I crawled onto the bed and silenced her protests with another scorching kiss. This time, she didn't even try to fight. Her hands dove into my hair, her fingers scraping my scalp while her legs wrapped around my waist, pulling me closer.

The need to fight the spell quickly dissolved until I couldn't remember why I shouldn't want this witch on a deeper, more permanent basis.

I trailed heated kisses along her jawline and down the column of her throat. "Just feel, petal. Stop resisting."

Bronwyn tilted her head back, eyes falling shut. "I don't...feel anything..."

My lips curved against her fluttering pulse. "Liar."

I nipped at the delicate skin, eliciting a breathy gasp.

"The spell.... Not me..."

I breathed in her rosy scent, intoxicating. "Keep telling yourself that."

My hands glided up to cup her breasts as my mouth continued its descent. Her breath hitched, back arching.

"You arrogant bas—" she cut off on a moan as I took a taut peak between my lips.

I lavished attention on one breast then the other, her hands fisting in my hair as she futilely tried to tug me back up.

"Smug jackass," she gasped out. "I'm not... enjoying this."

I raised my head to meet her lust-darkened gaze. "No? Then why are your lovely nipples hard for my mouth?"

A pretty flush stained her cheeks. "Fuck you."

"All in good time, petal." I winked before returning my attention lower.

My hands grasped her hips as I trailed kisses along her abdomen, my goal clear. She squirmed against the mattress, half-hearted protests falling from her lips, even as she widened her stance.

I slid off the bed, sinking to my knees before her, anticipation thrumming through me. Our game was nearing its peak.

"Just remember," I murmured against her silken skin, "you can lie to me, but you cannot lie to yourself…"

One flick of my tongue against her clit snapped my last grain of control. She groaned as I drove her to orgasm with a singular focus, abandoning all attempts at finesse. Between my fingers, lips, and tongue, she came screaming, her hands clawing at my hair, first pulling and then pushing, almost like she couldn't decide what she wanted.

Climbing back onto the bed, I hovered over her, trying fruitlessly to restrain myself. The second I notched my cock against her opening, something shot through me. A buzz of power maybe? It shot up my spine, setting off fireworks behind my eyes.

Bronwyn's head thrashed against the sheets while her back bowed.

A tiny spark of concern unfurled inside of me, but the rush of need silenced it before it could gain ground.

She lifted her hips, her feverish eyes fixed on me, her lips parted on a pant. She looked... lovely. Sprawled out beneath me, her cheeks rosy, her fiery hair cascading around her and her eyes glazed with lust. How had I missed this last time?

I slammed into her and she cried out. Those fireworks from before exploded into an inferno of sensation. It felt like my cock was encased in electricity, only it stroked me, squeezed and massaged until lasting more than a few seconds became increasingly unlikely.

With great effort, I stopped myself from pounding into her. She writhed beneath me, her head thrown back and her eyes squeezed shut.

"Are you okay?" I asked through gritted teeth.

She swallowed hard. "It wasn't like this last time."

"It might be the spell interacting with the bond."

Her eyes opened and she stared up at me, her stormy eyes soft for once. "Can you make it stop?"

Ordinarily, I wouldn't give an inch in someone else's favour. I would enjoy their misfortune, maybe stoke it. But with her staring at me like that, I might have done it, if I could.

Instead, I shook my head. The lust spell had to run its course, and I hadn't found a way to break the soul-bond yet. But I would.

I wanted to ask if she could handle the effects, but it would be pointless. Not even I had a chance. So instead, I tentatively pulled out.

The ripple effects from that one movement made my eyes roll back in my head and my balls draw tight. It didn't help that another orgasm shattered through Bronwyn, causing her to clamp down on me. I came on an agonised exhale, swearing as pleasure tore violently up my spine.

"How long is this going to last?" she asked, her voice strained.

"I don't know." It pained me to admit it.

Her brows furrowed, and I braced myself for some cutting remark while stiffening every muscle in my body to hold back the effects of the spell for a second, just a second, while we caught our breaths.

"Do you think it would leave us alone if we passed out from pleasure?"

For a second, all I could do was stare down at her, barely comprehending.

"Bloody hell, did that orgasm knock a few brain cells loose?" she snapped, her once soft eyes now spitting fire at me. "I'm telling you to fuck me so hard I black out. Can you handle that, or are you going to make us both suffer through this for the rest of the night?"

"What did I say about me being in charge?" I growled as I flipped her over onto her front. I pulled her back onto her knees and thrust back into her, gritting my teeth against the overpowering pulse of electric energy.

She squeaked as the spur above my cock pressed against her ass. From the sensations that flood me, it heightened the endless wave of pleasure.

"I think you're all talk." Her gasps grew louder with each pulse of my hips. "I bet you're nothing but a pussycat beneath that masochistic, demanding front."

A pussycat?

Absolute outrage roared through me. I'd show her a fucking pussycat.

I straightened up, gripping her hips tight, and pounded into her. I pushed the intoxicating beat of energy to the back of my mind, focusing on nothing but the way her body clutched at me, the way her cries grew more desperate with every second. It didn't take much to push her over the edge again, but to her dismay, she didn't pass out.

Round and round the cycles went, both of us orgasming so many times we lost count. Each time, the source of my power seemed to rejoice at the flush of power. An oddity I couldn't spare enough brain power to figure out. It had something to do with balancing her power, I knew that, but the rest of it? It escaped me and really, it didn't matter.

The spell clamped down on me, pushing all thought out and replacing it with one thought, one purpose. To fill her with so much cum, she had no other choice but to bear my child.

My power unfurled, sliding between us, caressing her skin and travelling down her body, pinching her nipples and circling her swollen nub. It pulsed, pinching the sensitive flesh, driving her over the edge again. I growled, pushing deeper into her, and overhead, the ceiling cracked as power leaked from me, from us. It didn't matter; I would rebuild the room as many times as it took.

I withdrew before thrusting back in, hitting her in a spot that made her moan again, my name falling from her lips like a curse and a prayer. Every time I filled her body with the chokehold of the spell, the consequences vibrated throughout my entire being, drowning out all else. It didn't even matter that it shook the ground beneath us — I lost myself in ecstasy, in her moans and gasps.

"Lucifer!" She screamed, her arms giving out. She fell to her elbows and pressed her face against the sheets. "I can't—"

"Yes, you can."

I didn't pause, leaning in to lap at the sweat beading on her neck, sucking a mark into her skin while my teeth ached with the need to bite her. Somehow, I resisted the pull of it, and instead forced her to come again in quick succession. She didn't fight, couldn't, as I pounded into her from behind, hungry for the power that coursed through her like an addictive drug.

The snarls I emitted, the growls of satisfaction, were a foreign language now, but they felt too good to stop.

I reached around, teasing her clit with my touch,

even as her body buckled and shuddered beneath me in one last, shattering orgasm. My name left her lips, a plea and a curse, as we both cried out in unison.

With a feral smile, I slammed into her, hoping that this would be the final time, emptying my seed within her, feeling her power pulse against me like a living thing.

Only it wasn't anywhere near the last time.

It took a full hour at a relentless pace before the pleasure became too much and exhaustion took us. But Bronwyn got her wish, she passed out, face-planting into a pillow. I turned her over before she could suffocate herself and she mumbled happily in her sleep, a tired smile claiming her lips.

What a strange witch.

Even stranger still: why did I suddenly want to bite her? I had lived for aeons and never felt that base urge towards another.

CHAPTER TWELVE

BRONWYN

*T*hree days later, and if I spent any more time in Lucifer's bed, I'd probably fuse with the damn sheets. I swear, Hell's got nothing on being the Devil's eternal booty call.

I tried to shuffle out once, hoping he'd fallen asleep, and I could slip away like some sneaky ninja, but Lucifer? Oh, he's got a sixth sense for that.

As soon as my pinky toe hit the perpetually hot floor, his eyes popped open. Like, come on, is there no escape?

If it couldn't get any worse, the goddess-damned

soulbond had gotten stronger with all the 'bonding time.'

I sighed loudly as he trailed hot kisses along my shoulder.

"Did you sneak another line into the contract about confining me to your bed?" I grumbled.

The last wave of the lust spell had started to weaken, and baseless hope unfurled inside of me. Followed swiftly by my determination. I would not spend another day locked in his room.

He chuckled, the sound igniting traitorous tingles along my spine. "Is my company truly so loathsome?"

I rolled over and shoved his roaming hands away. "You kidnapped me to be your supernatural baby machine. So yeah, buddy, snuggle time has lost its charm." I propped myself up on my elbows, meeting his gaze. "I'm not spending another day locked in this room. I can't."

He tensed before exhaling slowly. "I… apologise for the circumstance that brought you to Hell." Each word sounded dragged out by thumbscrews. "Perhaps a change of scenery might improve your mood."

My eyes narrowed suspiciously. "What, I get house arrest privileges now?"

He smiled, but it looked more like a grimace. "If

you promise to stay away from the Lords of Sins and not risk your life, yes."

"I didn't willingly do any of those things." I sat up and his gaze dropped to my naked breasts, the lust spell refusing to let him go. I covered myself and he tilted his head back, meeting my incredulous stare. "But I'm not going to look a gift horse in the mouth. Conjure me some clothes, and I'll be on my way."

His brow furrowed. "I didn't say you could go alone."

I shot him a sceptical look. "Oh, joy. Another guided tour of the Devil's Playground. That's exactly what I needed in my life."

Lucifer sighed, his frustration thinly veiled. "You're insufferable, you know that?"

"Coming from the guy who kidnapped me for his twisted reproduction plan, I'll take that as a compliment." I shook my head, my irritation bubbling to the surface. "Fine, let's get this over with. Show me the wonders of your personal Hell."

He rose from the bed and dressed himself with a flick of his fingers. I eyed him expectantly.

He stared at me, clearly missing the point. "What's the matter now?"

I let out an exasperated sigh. "Clothes, Lucifer. I

need something to wear that doesn't scream Devil's concubine."

He conjured an outfit, all frills and endless fabric. I glared at him. "Are you trying to make me look like a Victorian doll? Because I assure you, I won't survive Hell's heat in this."

"My apologies, Your Highness," Lucifer said, sarcasm dripping from the words.

His gaze moved over me, a glint of amusement finally piercing the lingering supernatural hunger and annoyance. With a graceful flourish of his hand, his power surged again, tingling against my far too sensitive skin.

"Is this more to your liking?"

The endless heavy fabrics melted away, replaced by flowing crimson layers. The dress grazed my ankles, lightweight material skimming my frame. It left my shoulders free while the sleeves teased my arms.

Turning before the mirror, I hardly recognised myself. The dress brought out rich highlights in my hair, almost giving my pale complexion a glow. Strange for a colour branding me as the Devil's consort. But I felt... nice. Beautiful even.

Which is stupid.

This was just another gilded cage of Lucifer's design, something to parade me around Hell in.

"Better," I said, shooting him a triumphant look.

A fleeting smirk played on his lips before he composed himself. He held out his hand. "Shall we?"

I stepped up to him, almost giddy with the thought of getting out. I didn't care where 'out' was as long as it wasn't here.

His hand wrapped around my waist. Too late, I remembered the last time he transported us. The room swirled sickeningly before reforming into blinding sunlight and powder soft sand.

I had a second to take in the dark palm trees swaying ominously in the hellish breeze before my stomach lurched violently. I doubled over just in time to spew my breakfast all over the black sand. Lucifer hovered awkwardly, patting my back.

Bet Gran could have handled that trip without tossing her cookies.

I wiped my mouth with a shaky hand as I straightened up. "Warn me next time."

"You have my word." He pulled me upright, dusting grains of sand from my dress.

Was that actual sincerity in his tone? But no, his tense expression stayed shuttered.

I snorted, taking in the black sky and flaming waves. "Something tells me your apologies don't come often or sincerely enough to recognise when they do."

His lips pursed. "I brought you to paradise, did I not? Very few guests of Hell get to see Inferna Palms."

The vast majority of those guests were damned souls and I highly doubted they got to choose which parts of this place they laid down their roots.

"Well, don't I feel special," I muttered, surveying the dark palm trees, the obsidian sands beneath my feet, and the demonic creatures lurking in the shadows. "Paradise still means white sand, crystal blue water and endless blue skies to me. This is some twisted Hell beach resort."

"Not quite." Lucifer smiled tightly. "This is my summer home."

I did not want to know what summer felt like in Hell. The current furnace was bad enough.

He led the way into a cabana suite next to the house. The pool awaited, its blood-red water flickering ominously.

"Seriously, does everything here have to scream deadly danger? That water looks like it'll peel my skin off on first contact!"

His throaty laughter surprised me. "It's enchanted to look deadly, but it won't harm your mortal body. Perfectly safe."

I hesitated, studying the pool again, trying to see

through the glamour to the reality beneath. Unfortunately, that had never been one of my strengths.

Glancing back at him, I waited for him to smirk or do something to give himself away. He didn't so much as react. He wasn't joking? No way was the Devil's private pool non-poisonous to humans. The temptation to soak all the aches he'd given me in the last few days beat at me.

What the hell, why not risk it?

"Well, in that case, got any enchanted swimsuits hidden around too?"

One wave of his hand later, I sported a snug red bikini. Before I could lose my nerve, I leapt off the side of the pool. The warm water wrapped around me, fizzing in a pleasant way.

I surfaced to find Lucifer staring at the space where I had been, a strange mix of bewilderment and need flickering across his face.

A warm flush burned through me. I liked it.

CHAPTER THIRTEEN

BRONWYN

"Quite a view, isn't it?" Lucifer said.

He reclined next to me on a sun lounger, seemingly at ease in his infernal paradise.

The scent of sulphur lingered in the air. Hell's sun dipped lower in the sky, casting a surreal glow over the landscape. I squinted against the reddish light, marvelling still at the fact Hell had a sun. He had tried to explain it to me but it went straight over my head. I snorted, eyeing the demonic landscape, more relaxed than I'd felt in a long time. "If you're into the whole 'fire and brimstone' aesthetic, sure."

He chuckled, a low sound that resonated through me. "You mortals and your aesthetic preferences. Always demanding paradise, yet never satisfied."

We had nearly reached the sixth hour and already I could feel the effects of the lust spell getting ready to strike. Not yet. Please, not yet. I wanted to enjoy this rare moment of semi-normalcy as long as I could.

I leaned back on the lounger, feeling the cool fabric against my skin. "Well, you're the one who brought me to your twisted version of paradise. What does that say about you?"

He raised a brow, a smirk playing on his lips. "Perhaps I enjoy keeping you on your toes."

"You enjoy a lot of things, it seems. Kidnapping witches, torturing souls, and now, playing tour guide."

Lucifer sighed. "Such a succinct summary of my existence. You wound me, Bronwyn."

I smirked. "You're the Devil. I'm sure you'll survive." I turned to face him, my expression turning serious. "Speaking of you being the all scary Devil, why did you have to resort to trickery to get a witch to give you a child? Couldn't charm your way into a willing partnership? Or conjure your own mini-Lucifers with a thought?"

Surprise crossed his elegant features before his

expression shut down. It was a personal question, and I knew it, but I needed to understand.

The longer I watched, the longer I waited, the more that mask cracked.

Eventually, he sighed. "There are balances to be maintained, even in Hell. The Morrigan struck a deal with me to restore equilibrium. I was required to produce an heir with a witch, but she's harder to bargain with than me."

A half-smile tugged at his lips, there and gone in the blink of an eye. So the Devil did have a sense of humour.

"It wasn't until the ink had dried that I realised she'd added a stipulation." He met my gaze, his serious expression and tone making my breath freeze in my lungs. "The heir had to come from an Owen witch. No other bloodline would do."

"But why?"

"The Morrigan kept her reasoning well-guarded. All I know is that there's power in the Owen bloodline, so I've always assumed it was a matter of using it to restore the balance."

I snorted, unable to keep my disbelief to myself. "Power? Yeah right. Every time I unleash my so-called power, it turns into a chaotic circus." I shook my head. "The fact I was able to summon you was a fluke."

Silence fell and I glanced over at the Devil. He studied me, like I was a dragon that didn't know how to fly.

"What?"

"You're not underpowered."

"Yes, I am," I said, my voice flat despite the ridiculousness of his claims.

"Who told you such a ridiculous lie?"

I scowled. "No one had to tell me anything. I failed my coven entry test. Wasn't powerful enough."

Lucifer's laughter rang out, surprising and jarring.

"What's so funny about that?"

He composed himself, a wry smile lingering. "The idea of you being underpowered. Your ancestors were feared among demons. They were the only witches able to summon me, the only ones capable of sending a demon back to hell with a mere look and a muttered word."

I sat there, stunned, absorbing the revelation. "What happened to me, then? Why don't I have that power?"

His gaze softened, and he explained, "It's not about lacking power, it's about not knowing how to use it. You leak emotions in a way no Owen witch would dare around a demon. It leaves you vulnerable."

"Why didn't my grandmother train me properly?

How could I appear underpowered to the coven when I'm not?"

"Perhaps she had her reasons. But it's not too late to learn, Bronwyn. I can teach you."

The offer lingered between us, but I couldn't bring myself to accept. Not yet. How could I escape if I were wrapped up in favours to the Devil?

I changed the subject as the sun dipped lower.

"Even before the contract, were there no women in your life who would have taken offence to you being effectively forced to have a kid with someone else? What about family?"

For a moment, his eyes glazed over as he stared up at the sky. Pain flickered through our bond, gone quick as lightning. But I caught flashing glimpses of screaming, feathers burnt black, beloved faces contorting in disgusted rage...

"I fell from Heaven, Bronwyn." Loneliness crushed my ribs, echoing back from him. "I lost everything. Family, companionship. I've been alone for a very long time."

I swallowed, my bravado momentarily slipping away. "Yeah," I whispered, almost to myself. "I know that feeling."

Gran was my last family too before she passed. No coven would accept this chaos-cursed disappointment.

How long had it been since someone knew the real me beneath the sarcasm and steel backbone?

"Lucifer…" His name fell softly from my lips, my voice hoarse with both of our pain.

Without thinking, I reached for him. Not because of a spell, but to comfort. I placed my hand over his, squeezing in the only way I knew how.

"It's their loss, you know." I swept my free hand vaguely skyward.

And oddly, I meant it.

His hand turned under mine, tentatively threading our fingers together.

CHAPTER FOURTEEN

LUCIFER

*B*ronwyn's small hand rested in mine. Something so human, so simple as a touch, shouldn't have affected me, but it stirred something within the heart I thought long dead.

I had lived for aeons, seen civilisations rise and fall. But this moment, this small, tender connection with a witch who should have been cunning enough to avoid crossing my path, felt like a deviation from the norms of my existence.

The obsidian-black leaves of the palm trees rustled with an eerie wind, their shadows dancing over the cabana's sinister architecture. The sun lazily crept towards the horizon, and creatures awoke in the forest behind the house. I could feel them stretching in their dens, my nocturnum drakes, serpent-dragon hybrids, and the shadowstalkers, predators crafted for Inferna Palms, their ink-black fur blending seamlessly into the darkness. Hunger for blood coursed through their minds.

Ignoring them all, I studied Bronwyn's profile.

She had no idea what she did to me. How could she, when I could barely fathom it?

What possessed me to bring her to my secret paradise, I couldn't say. I never shared this space with anyone, not even my inner circle. But when she'd narrowed those fierce, stubborn eyes on me, the words had formed themselves.

Couldn't say I regretted it. Instead, I found myself lost in an unexpected moment of peace. An oddity that I… enjoyed.

"So this is how the Devil unwinds, hmm?" she said. "Lounging in a tropical cabana overlooking your demonic kingdom?"

"I'll have you know I work exceptionally hard torturing the souls of the damned." My grip tightened on her hand, almost like some part of me feared she would take it away. "I'm entitled to a little downtime now and then."

She snorted. "Somehow I have a hard time picturing you doing manual labour. Don't you have minions for that?"

Her laughter, light and unforced, pierced the ever-present darkness of my realm. It was a sound so foreign in this place, yet it resonated within me, a reminder of something I hadn't felt in millennia.

"I'm hands on when required. Though I'll admit, I prefer to delegate." I smiled, uncharacteristically trying to soften the gruesomeness of my words. "Torture can be rather unimaginative at times. I find psychological torment is often more effective."

Her brows quirked. "Remind me not to get on your bad side."

A shadow passed over her face and she turned pensive, picking at a loose thread on the lounge chair.

"What is it?"

"How did you cope with... you know, after the fall?" she asked, her tone careful but laced with genuine curiosity rather than the usual sarcasm, "Rebuilding everything from scratch?"

I released a slow breath, staring up at the garish sky. It was not a topic I cared to dwell on. "Through spite, I suppose."

Her gaze softened, and she leaned closer. "That's a bit... bleak, isn't it?"

"Perhaps, but it fuelled a purpose." I shrugged, trying for an unaffected air I never felt when thinking of my plummet to Hell. "After the fall, everything I had known was stripped away. I was cast out, betrayed. While wallowing in that betrayal, I discovered a determination I hadn't known existed within me. I was consumed with rage over the injustice, determined to prove I could build a kingdom to rival the Silver City in splendour and power."

Memories of the Silver City filled my mind with its piercing grace and the choirs of angels in rapturous song. It had shone, holy and whole, under our Creator's light. A pang of loss lanced through me.

She searched my gaze. "You turned your fall into a beginning, not an end."

I nodded. "But rebuilding wasn't just about creating a realm; it was about forging a new identity, one that defied those who cast me aside. I carved order from chaos through sheer force of will. Moulded the darkness into my vision. But it was many centuries before Hell resembled anything close to a functioning realm."

Awe flickered in her eyes, so subtle, yet my breath caught.

"When all I knew was grace and divine light, to subsist in shadow and fire took immense adaptation. I discovered strengths I never needed before."

I met Bronwyn's eyes, struck by the empathy there. *Does she realise she's softening towards me?*

"In truth, determination and resilience were key. Imagination, also, to build something beautiful from such corruption." I gestured around us. "Even Inferna Palms, dark as it is, stands testament to that creativity."

She smiled. "Sounds like you reinvented yourself."

"It was that or succumb to oblivion." I shrugged, an attempt to downplay what I had endured. "I chose to rise, to make a kingdom from the ashes of my disgrace. It was... a form of rebellion, a way to prove my worth outside the confines of Heaven."

"I never thought about it that way." She nodded slowly, a thoughtful glint in her eyes. "You didn't just accept your fate; you reshaped it."

Her simple words echoed within me. Had anyone ever recognised that aspect of my journey? It wasn't only about defiance or anger; it was about reclaiming a sense of self in a universe that seemed determined to break me.

"Yes," I said, awe deepening my voice. I had never been able to give voice to these memories without destroying something. How had she changed that in such a short time? "It was a... transformative time. I learned the hard way that even in the darkest of places, one can find a way to thrive."

She swallowed, glancing away, but not before I spotted the shine of tears in her eyes. Was it for my trials or the echo of her own?

"It was worth everything, to have that freedom," I continued quietly. "To form my own thoughts, my own destiny. I would make the same choice again." Disconcerting pride unfurled in my chest as she straightened her shoulders and met my gaze with a hard determination. "So in the end, it was defiance that built this empire." I smirked. "To prove I could rise higher the second time."

She rolled her eyes. "Why am I not surprised the Devil thrives on spite?"

I smiled. For the first time, I had bared my true self without judgement. With this bold witch, I need not pretend to be anything but myself. A liberating realisation, and one I wished could last an eternity.

"Never thought there'd be perks to getting soulbound to the Devil," Bronwyn said a little while later.

Her laughter was infectious, yet as it faded, a pensive expression took its place.

Not for the first time, I wondered how much our mystical bond influenced her attitude towards me. Did it compel this rapport between us? This illusion of understanding? I had lived a solitary existence for so long, trust and affection were foreign concepts. It was easier to believe our connection was simply manufactured magic, sparing myself the vulnerability of hoping for something real.

My doubts must have shown, for she tilted her head and asked, "What is it?"

"Do you ever wonder if your comfort around me is genuine, or if it's the bond pulling the strings?"

"I don't know. Probably a bit of both, if I'm being honest." She lifted her eyes to mine, vibrant despite the gloom. "But that doesn't make it any less real."

I absorbed this, turning the statement over in my mind. Trying to parse where the mystical ended and the authentic began. A question with no simple answer, it would seem.

Bronwyn took a shuddering breath, her voice

growing thick. "You remind me of her sometimes. My Gran. She had that same glint in her eye when she was conniving some bit of mischief." A watery chuckle escaped her. "Drove the coven spare with her antics. But she cared for me when no one else did."

Maybe it was her pain that spoke to me. Or the loneliness of being branded an outcast by her own kind.

"You possess a strength few can comprehend." On impulse, I reached to brush a tear from her cheek. At that moment, she was neither witch nor rival, merely a young woman weighed down with grief, weary of betrayal, and aching for someone to see the truth of her. And despite myself, I found I cared. A revelation that left me shaken, unsure of how to proceed.

I withdrew my hand, the moment broken. Twilight had stolen over Inferna Palms and soon the creatures of the night would emerge to prowl.

Once I would have enjoyed my creatures' reign of terror, the symphony of shrieks as they pursued helpless souls. Now the thought of exposing Bronwyn to that, her defiance giving way to fear, grated against my mind like a discordant note.

When had I become so altered, that I wished to shield this bold witch from the true horrors of my domain?

It was a conundrum, yet I could not deny the truth — she had awoken in me an instinct to protect. I didn't care if it was a weakness; I would keep her from harm's reach, even in the bowels of Hell.

"I should probably take you somewhere less... foreboding."

I glanced towards the darkening sky, stars flickering deceivingly above the water.

Bronwyn followed my gaze, her smirk returning. "What, the Devil scared of a little local wildlife?"

I chuckled. "Not for myself, of course. But you, my petal, are not quite equipped to handle what lurks in these shadows."

Her eyes twinkled. "Then lead the way."

I stood, offering her my hand. She took it without hesitation and I led her up the winding path to my villa. As much as I tried to silence the incessant questions, I couldn't. Were her reactions to me sincere? Did she walk willingly at my side, or was the soulbond compelling her compliance? Her witty banter could simply be a facade, masking a repulsion she was magically bound to suppress.

I studied her from the corner of my eye — the defiant lift of her chin, the nonchalance with which she met the nightmarish landscape. Perhaps her spirit was simply stronger than I realised, able to weather the darkness I cloaked myself in.

But I had to be certain. As we reached the imposing double doors, I made a silent vow — I would find a way to break our bond, if she permitted it. Only then could I know her feelings were freely given, not products of The Morrigan's magic.

Even if it meant losing her, I must give Bronwyn back her freedom of choice.

CHAPTER FIFTEEN

LUCIFER

*T*he next day, I walked into the library in my wing to resume my hunt for a spell that would successfully sever the bond between us. Musical chanting gave me pause.

I slipped soundlessly through the doors, intrigued and mildly annoyed that someone dared enter my wings unannounced.

Instead of an intruder, I found Bronwyn, surrounded by an array of meticulously drawn chalk circles, candles flickering in eerie unison.

The air shimmered with the arcane energy she

harnessed, and for a moment, I forgot why I entered the library. I forgot my need to free us both.

Instead, I found myself captivated by her beauty, the way her fiery hair fluttered on the waves of power leaking from her, the glow of her skin. The flickering candlelight accentuated the delicate curve of her cheek, the determined set of her jaw.

It was unlikely that her spell, meant to resurrect her grandmother, would be successful here, yet watching her, I couldn't convince myself to step forward and stop her.

The lust spell had ceased its torment, yet my fingers itched to touch her, to worship her body. A stark contrast to the disgust I usually reserved for mortals. In a few weeks, my usual repulsion for her kind had melted away.

Or maybe that was only true in her case.

A boom sounded, and the circle erupted in flames. Instinct kicked in, and without a second thought, I surged forward, snatching Bronwyn out of the path of the fire. The heat lashed against my skin as I contained the flames, extinguishing the volatile magic that threatened to consume the room.

She stumbled away from me, her eyes wide with shock and fear. But instead of gratitude, anger surged through her. She slammed her hands against my chest, each hit resonating with a mixture of frustration and confusion.

"You gave me a bad spell!" Her words cut through the air, filled with accusation and a hint of desperation. "You tricked me."

"The spell was designed for Earth, not Hell." I caught her hands, stopping her from pounding them into my chest. I watched in horrified silence as the strong-willed witch crumpled, tears streaming down her face. It was a sight I hadn't expected, and a disconcerting twist settled in my gut.

Acting on some long rusty instinct, I pulled her into my chest again and held her.

"Hush now," I murmured, keeping my voice low. "You're unharmed. It'll all be okay." I smoothed back wild curls.

Had she always been so small, so fragile in my arms? So very breakable?

"But it won't. I can't work the spell. I can't bring her back," she mumbled around her sobs.

She buried her face against my chest, her hands fisting the fabric of my shirt, her tears soaking into the fabric. Her knees buckled and I went down with her, lowering her gently to the floor. Each shuddering breath reverberated through her entire being, taking a piece of me with it.

"This isn't me," she whispered, her voice muffled against my chest. "I don't cry. Ever. What's happening to me?"

"The lust spell has calmed, hasn't it?"

She nodded, sniffling.

"Its effects would only ease when…" I trailed off, but comprehension was already dawning in her stormy eyes.

"When I get pregnant," she finished bitterly.

Bronwyn pulled away, scrubbing the tears from her cheeks angrily as she scrambled to her feet and backed away. "This is your fault! If you hadn't tricked me—"

"You know I had no more choice in this than you did," I said, keeping my voice calm and level, though her accusation stung for some unfathomable reason. "The magics of the contract—"

"Just stop!" she shouted, fresh tears welling. "I don't want your excuses or explanations. I want my grandmother back!"

Her grief pierced me, and I rose, approaching her as one might a wounded animal. She shouted at me, calling me every name under the infernal sun. "You've messed up everything. My magic, my grandmother — everything!"

A sigh escaped my lips. "I didn't anticipate any of—"

"I don't care what you anticipated! I want solutions, not excuses."

I took a step towards her, my hands out at my side. "Look," I said, my tone softer, "I can find your grandmother. I may not know her exact location, but I can find her."

She blinked, surprise flickering in her tear-filled eyes. "Why? You said you couldn't before."

"It takes a lot of power to trace a soul."

She regarded me with suspicion.

"Consider it... payment for the pain I've brought you."

"That's not an answer." She squared her shoulders, fiery temper returning. "Admit it — you lied about not knowing where she was. You've had her soul all along."

I held up a placating hand. "Believe me, if your grandmother were here, I would return her to ease your suffering. But she is beyond even my reach currently."

"I don't believe you. Tell me the truth!"

"I have this peculiar need to make you happy!" I shouted back, frustrated and finally understanding what drove mortal men to drink so much. "Are you pleased now? You've forced The Devil to admit he feels."

Shock silenced her for a breath. Then she whispered, "Why would you want to make me happy?"

I faltered, unsure how to explain the foreign emotions swirling inside of me.

"I don't know. Consider it another consequence of our agreement." I searched her face, noting the moment her anger fizzled out. "If I find your grandmother, your suffering will ease. I see no advantage in seeing you in pain."

She frowned, as if trying to decipher some complex puzzle. "But you're the Devil. Your kind thrives on pain and suffering."

"Not your pain and suffering," I whispered, having no idea where the words came from but knowing they were right. "If it helps, I'll swear another blood oath, whatever you require to accept that I mean every word and stop the tears." Desperation tinged my voice. She swiped at her wet eyes, her cheeks reddening. "I will find your grandmother's soul, no matter where she is hidden. This I vow to you."

My nail transformed into a claw and I held it to my palm to make the oath.

"No." She rushed forward, catching my hand before I could draw blood. "That won't be necessary. I believe you. I'll take your word, though I have no idea why you're suddenly so intent on helping me," she whispered the last part, staring into my eyes, her body so close her heat brushed against mine.

The lust spell had broken. I could feel it in my bones. Why then did I feel this intense need for her? My appetite for her appeared to be insatiable still and this drive to please her... it was an alien experience.

I'd gotten what I wanted. I would have an heir. My domain would grow in power. It should be enough.

CHAPTER SIXTEEN

BRONWYN

A week had passed since the lust spell released its hold. After my meltdown over the resurrection spell failing, I'd expected him to retreat. He had his heir, after all — why tolerate my presence further when all he needed to do was wrap me up in cotton wool and wait?

Instead, I spent my nights in Lucifer's bed and my days digging through every nook and cranny of his wing. He grew more affectionate with each passing day.

Once I'd stopped crying that day, he'd drawn me a bath.

The next morning, I woke to find my favourite

caramelised hazelnut muffins waiting at breakfast. And last night, he'd presented me with armfuls of books from my childhood, conjured from thin air, before he added an extension to his library with every book I'd ever thought about reading.

He pulled me close, nuzzling into my hair with a contented sigh. How could this be the same proud fallen angel who needed a lust spell to touch me? Who tried to kill me the moment he realised he had been eternally bound to me? I still struggled to reconcile the two.

"Sleep well, little witch?" he drawled, his voice rumbling beneath my ear.

I hummed affirmation, letting myself relax into his arms. He traced lazy patterns on my skin, innocent and intimate all at once. It was disconcerting and pleasing, a strange mix, just like my feelings about our situation.

I still wanted to go home. Or more to the point, I wanted to perform the resurrection spell and get my grandmother back. But that would mean leaving him.

I should keep my distance. Developing real feelings for him would be another cog in the insanity of this place. But with each passing day, my defences crumbled further. I found myself watching his face, memorising each expression that crossed it. Had his smiles always been so gentle? His eyes so full of buried longing?

He absently twisted a lock of my hair around his finger. Such a simple gesture, yet it made my heart flip and my breath still, waiting to see what he'd do next.

What if it was too late? What if I'd already fallen for him?

If I didn't want to leave anymore, what did that mean for our plan to break the soulbond and send me home after the baby was born?

What did I have to go home to? I had no friends. I hated the house in the middle of the woods as much as my ancestors had loved it. My grandmother's coven had never been kind to me.

My future sprawled out in my mind's eye and it was bleak. All I'd have was work. I would spend my days working in a small corner shop in town, and spend my nights alone with nothing but my books. All while my child grew up in hell.

If he could find my grandmother, why would I ever want to return to the mortal world?

Mortal world. Goddess, he was rubbing off on me.

But truthfully, if given the choice, I wouldn't want to. I would choose to spend my eternity, however long it should be, in hell, with my family… with the man I loved.

I froze, the realisation crashing over me.

There was no question of if. I did. I loved him. Against all reason, I had fallen for the Devil.

My heart raced. What the hell was I thinking? Loving Lucifer went against every rule of survival I'd ever learned. He was fire — beautiful, but one wrong move could mean death.

"Are you well, petal?" Lucifer asked, concern lacing his tone as he sat up, forcing me on to my back while he peered down at me. "Is it the child?" His hand fell to my stomach, heating as he checked on it.

"I'm fine. It's fine." I caressed his cheek, willing him to believe me.

"Then why is your heart racing?"

"I — I just had a sudden memory of being chased through the halls." I gripped the nape of his neck and tugged him down to me, smiling like I wasn't making life-altering decisions. "I'm fine."

He didn't believe me, but I didn't give him a chance to question me further. I kissed him hard, coaxing him to respond until he let it go.

Even knowing the risk, I couldn't tear myself away from him. I was a moth to his flame. This went far beyond physical attraction. His smiles, his laughter, the way he knew how to comfort me — they anchored me to him as strongly as the soulbond itself.

And if I loved him, he must feel the same. Why else the effortless affection each morning, as if we'd woken beside each other for years? The constant gifts, the hours spent discussing anything and everything?

No, his actions could mean only one thing: the Devil loved me in return.

Impossible yet undeniable.

The kiss deepened, quickly turning heated, and I let the concern float away to be dealt another day. The taste of his lips consumed me, pushing out all other thoughts. My fingers tangled in his dark locks, pulling him closer as our bodies moved in sync, our desire growing with each passing second.

His hands swept down my body with a possessiveness that made my heart race all over again. My skin burned beneath his touch, craving more of him.

His fingers delved between my thighs, finding me already wet for him. He groaned into my mouth, and his pleasure beat at me through the bond.

"Do you want me, little witch?"

I could only nod, my breath hitching as his fingers expertly circled my clit. I arched my back, pushing myself further into his touch, desperate for more. He pumped his fingers in and out of me, making me writhe against him as I let out a string of moans and gasps.

Needing to hold on to something, anything, to stop my world from spinning off its axis, I blindly reached out. My fingers grazed Lucifer's wing. The feathers were softer than I imagined, like the most luxurious velvet but way cooler. Unable to help myself, I petted them, marvelling at how something belonging to Hell's CEO could feel so... divine.

He groaned as I stroked them, a sound that sank beneath my skin and worked its way down my spine.

"You need to stop doing that," he said, his voice hoarse.

I glanced at him from the corner of my eye. "Were they always this soft?"

"Yes," he forced out through gritted teeth. "But they got more sensitive when I fell so unless you want this to end too soon, stop."

I laughed. As if I'd believe a little petting of some feathers could get him off and stop him from getting it up again in a blink. He'd fucked me into the mattress back to back enough times for me to know that last part was a complete exaggeration on his part.

But the first... now that merited investigation.

With my gaze firmly fixed on him, I dragged my nails across the ridge of his wing. His reaction was instant, eyes lowering to half-mast, neck tensing so the tendons stood out, that delicious groan that did delightful things to me.

"Bronwyn," he growled. "I warned you."

His power surged forward, wrapping around my wrists and hoisting my arms up and over my head to rest against the pillows. I tugged experimentally and his power tugged back.

I stared up at him, my mouth agape. Yes, he'd warned me but I didn't think it would take such a... kinky turn.

An unrestrained grin stretched my lips. "Clearly, I haven't searched hard enough. Where are you hiding the pleasure room?"

He shook his head and ignored my teasing. Instead, he focused his attention back on the apex of my thighs.

This time he stroked me with not only his fingers but his power. I'd never imaged energy could take form, but oh did Lucifer find a way. It spiralled inside of me, caressing my walls while he played with my clit.

My nails dug into the palms of my hands as he drove me to the edge and pushed me over. The orgasm crashed through my body, causing me to grip onto his shoulders for dear life.

Spent, I collapsed back against the mattress, but he didn't slow. He continued to move his fingers inside me, to flick his power against every sensitive nerve-ending I had, drawing out my pleasure until I couldn't take it anymore. I whimpered, begging for mercy, as my body convulsed with the aftershocks of my release.

"That's just the start, petal," he purred. "You can do so much better."

Lucifer moved on top of me, his weight pressing me into the mattress. Grasping me behind the knees, he tugged me forward, his movements demanding and commanding.

With his cock nudging at my entrance, he stopped. His eyes locked with mine, filled with a mixture of desire and possessiveness.

"Tell me, Bronwyn," he murmured, his words sending shivers down my spine. "Tell me that you're mine."

I nodded, unable to form the words. But he didn't move.

"Say it," he growled, his voice dripping with desire. "Say you're mine."

I gazed up into Lucifer's smouldering eyes, the intensity of his gaze piercing through my soul. How was I meant to read this as anything else but his love?

"I'm yours," I whispered, my voice trembling.

Satisfaction flickered across his face before he surged forward, thrusting himself into me with a force that stole my breath away.

CHAPTER SEVENTEEN

BRONWYN

"*T*here you are. Your timing is perfect."

Lucifer smiled at me as I walked into his study the next day, barely pausing in his scribbling. I edged closer, eying the arcane symbols he chalked onto the floor and walls. *Why the walls?* Candles and crystals splayed out at strategic points in a more recognisable manner. Dark, ancient books lay open on the desk, discoloured pages fluttering.

I frowned at the occult items. "What's all this for?"

He set down a bundle of sage, brushing his hands off. "I've finally gathered everything we need for the ritual." His eyes glinted. "To break our soulbond."

My heart stuttered. The words circled inside my mind on repeat. I kept hoping I'd misheard, but he continued setting up the ritual without another glance my way.

Was that what he really wanted?

I couldn't wrap my head around it. How could he possibly want to break our bond? I couldn't tear my gaze away from him, even as doubts gnawed at my soul. He looked so focused, so determined. It was both mesmerising and frightening to witness.

He turned to face me, a knowing smile playing at the corners of his lips. "Don't worry, petal. Once this ritual is complete, everything will be as it was before, except we'll be free from this binding."

With my heart in my throat, I approached the desk and he reached for me, his hands falling to my hips as he helped me onto the surface. The grip of his fingers sent a rush of memories flooding my mind — all the ways he'd held me in the last two weeks.

I lay down and he began the incantation. I studied his face, barely hearing the words as I tried to decipher the emotions in his eyes. He'd shielded himself from me, making it next to impossible for me to read him.

A dull ache started in my chest and I winced as it intensified. Lucifer didn't notice. He kept chanting, his attention fixed on the book beside me. Lines formed in his brow as he invoked the spell, speaking each word with focused precision.

Was this supposed to hurt?

The ache spread, deepened, until a searing pain circled my heart. I whimpered, shifting helplessly on the desk, as if I could escape it. He didn't so much as falter in his incantation or glance at me in question. Sweat beaded on my forehead and it took everything I had to keep my eyes open and my mind aware. For all the good it did.

A blinding light erupted above me, flooding the room with stark white, forcing all of the dark reds, blacks and greens to fade to almost nothing. It felt like time froze but in reality only seconds passed before it arrowed into me. I gasped, unable to contain the sharp, visceral pain.

He'd said it would free us from the binding, not tear at the very essence of my being.

"Stop!" I screamed.

He finally looked at me, his eyes widening with horror and a flash of what could have been regret, but definitely not love. Had I imagined it all along?

The pain was endless. My vision blurred, the edges blackening as the spell dug into me, clawing at my heart. I clutched at my chest, expecting to find it wet with blood. Thankfully, nothing but fabric grazed my fingers, not that it mattered when the power burrowed into my chest. An agonised scream tore up my throat.

Another surge of pain, sharper and more profound, radiated from my chest. My entire body convulsed, and I screamed, the sound echoing in the walls of Lucifer's study.

Suddenly, it all stopped — the pain, the questions, the confusion. Blissful silence surrounded me as the darkness crawled in and I welcomed it.

LUCIFER

Desperation clawed at the edges of my carefully maintained composure. This wasn't how it was supposed to go. The sounds and sight of her convulsing in pain lanced my heart, evoking unfamiliar regret. I, who revelled in suffering, despised inflicting it upon her.

Our eyes locked, and in that moment, I saw. The pain tearing at her was beyond anything she could have handled.

But there was something worse than even that.

Doubt.

She doubted me. Whether I would purposefully put her through a ritual that might kill her. And... I couldn't answer it, I couldn't reassure her, because I doubted myself too.

I halted the ritual, but the damage had already taken root. I attempted to reverse the spell, to pull back the threads that ensnared her. But the darkness had already claimed her, and the shadows deepened around us.

The room fell silent. The only sounds were the lingering echoes of her screams. That sound would haunt my nightmares for eternity.

I stared at her motionless form. The pain had stopped, but so had everything else. I couldn't feel her with my power and the once vibrant bond had fallen silent in my chest.

My hands trembled as I touched her cheek, her neck, searching for a pulse. Panic surged through me, a feeling I hadn't experienced in centuries.

"Bronwyn!" Gripping her shoulders, I shook her, as if that would help. "Wake up!"

Her eyes remained open, their stormy grey now dulled and vacant.

"No," I muttered, my voice strained. "This wasn't supposed to happen."

I cradled her lifeless body against my chest, the situation settling on me like a heavy shroud.

This was my fault.

My fingers traced over her cooling skin while I watched in despair as her soul began to slip away. A spectral wisp, ethereal and fragile, rose from her chest.

An unfamiliar wetness slid down my cheeks, and it took a moment to register — tears.

"You can't leave me," I whispered, the words a desperate plea. "I won't allow it."

Her soul, a wisp of ethereal beauty, danced at the edge of my grasp. I was meant to be this great and powerful being.

I let my power go, let it plunge into her, let it force her heart to pump, her lungs to draw air and her blood to circulate.

I drew hard from the Core, pulling more power than I ever had. The very essence that defined me, that made me the ruler of Hell, surged through my veins. With a force beyond mortal comprehension, I reached for her departing soul and caught it.

My hands shook as I channelled more into her, willing her soul to reconnect with her body. It was like trying to reignite a star long burnt out, an act of futility and despair.

"Stay with me," I pleaded, each word a command, yet laced with an unfamiliar desperation.

Fear clawed at me. A part of me, a part I never knew existed, was fracturing, a million shards of agony.

"Bronwyn, please," I whispered, my voice breaking, a sound foreign to my ears.

Her body remained still, lifeless, a hollow shell where once a fierce spirit resided.

In a moment of desperation, I called out to the one being I never thought I would seek aid from. Not after she'd caused this mess.

"Morrigan!" My shout was more accusation than plea, a bitter outcry to the goddess who had orchestrated this cruel farce. "You see this? Look at what your meddling has done!"

I glared into the shadows, half expecting, half hoping for her to materialise, to face the chaos she'd sown. But there was nothing, only the oppressive silence of my own domain, mocking me.

"If she dies, it's on you!" My voice was laced with fury and contempt. "Your bloody games, your twisted conditions! You wanted an heir from an Owen witch? Look where your whims have led us.

"You wanted to bind me to her, to entangle our fates. Well, congratulations," I spat out the words, my gaze fixed on the ceiling.

Somehow I knew she wouldn't respond. Still, the silence was relentless, eating at me while I slowly lost my mind to grief.

"You're supposed to be a goddess of witches. You drew us together, you bound our souls for your own purpose, and now, as she teeters on the brink, you turn your back. What kind of goddess forsakes her own?" My voice thundered across the void, a challenge thrown to the unseen deity. "No wonder they cast you aside like the useless figurehead you are."

Silence followed my rant, and a bitter truth settled in my heart. I loved her. I loved Bronwyn. The realisation hit me like a blow, staggering in its intensity. I, the embodiment of pride and power, brought to my knees by love. A love that had crept into my being, insidious and undeniable.

"I'll give you anything," I whispered, my voice as broken as my heart.

Silence engulfed the room, but the shadows around us came alive, cackling at my desperation. Still I waited, something indescribable filling me. Hope? It was as if a dam had broken inside me, releasing a flood of emotions I had long since forgotten or buried under layers of cynicism and pride.

Then, something shifted.

It was subtle, a mere whisper of change in the air.

A tingling energy prickled my senses, faint at first. It unfurled like a dormant flower inside of her. I gasped as it wove into mine. Our energies melded in an intimate dance, no longer two separate forces but a unified blaze.

Bronwyn remained still, yet her power now crackled through our bond. It caressed my essence, beseeching me to guide it. To command it as I willed.

I tightened my hold on her limp body. Her life force surged under my direction, flooding her veins, jump-starting her vital organs.

A faint pulse throbbed under my fingertips. I inhaled sharply, focusing every shred of my infernal senses. Had I imagined it?

No — there it was again, stronger now.

Relief crashed over me, making my hands shake. I pressed a palm to her breastbone, concentrating on the delicate flicker of life within her. With each pulse, a bit more colour returned to her ashen cheeks.

Her heart sputtered, then caught a steady rhythm. Lungs expanded with sweet, precious breath. The sound was sweeter than a siren's song.

I stroked her hair, marvelling at the vibrant connection humming between us. Our magics continued their hypnotic dance, now flowing as one.

She was alive. Nothing else mattered, not my

wounded pride, not the possibility that she might hate me. Bronwyn would continue drawing breath, would keep challenging and surprising me with her mortal mind.

And I would savour every precious moment fate granted us.

CHAPTER EIGHTEEN

BRONWYN

I woke in Lucifer's bed, alone, the red-tinged morning light filtering through the curtains, and for a blissful moment, I thought it was just another morning, that it had all been a dream.

Lucifer sprawled in an armchair by the side of the bed, his feet propped on the mattress while his head lolled forward, his chin resting on his chest. He looked so adorable like that, but there were lines around his eyes and a streak of white in his hair I'd never seen before, almost like he'd aged a decade overnight.

Why isn't he in bed?

I shifted, thinking to go to him. My body ached

from head to toe in response and reality hit me like a sledgehammer — the ritual, the heartbreak, the pain, the determined expression on Lucifer's face — and a horrified sound escaped my lips.

He jolted awake, on his feet in an instant, and rushed to my side. "What's wrong?" His hand came to my cheek, his eyes searching mine urgently. "Does something hurt?"

I shook my head, leaning unconsciously into his touch. The familiar heat of it steadied me.

But only for a second. The panic receded, leaving behind the telltale ache of heartbreak. I'd been such an idiot, projecting feelings onto Lucifer that he clearly didn't share. Of course the Devil couldn't love anyone, let alone a witch like me.

It was all an illusion. A twisted byproduct of the lust spell, nothing more. His main concern was producing an heir. Any affection was merely a means to that end.

What about the baby?

My hands fell to my stomach as a new sense of loss invaded my body. It wasn't a baby yet, just a cluster of cells, but no way could it have survived that much pain.

"It's okay. I pulled you back fast enough to save it," he said.

I nodded in acknowledgement, not trusting my

voice not to crack or betray me more than my heart had.

If I died, his chance of fulfilling his agreement to The Morrigan died with me. I was missing something, some key piece that would make all of this chaos fall into place. But my mind felt sluggish, still hazy with the aftereffects of the spell and the sting of heartbreak.

I needed time. Time away from Lucifer and his inscrutable motivations. Time to heal and rebuild my shattered walls before determining my next move.

Had the spell even worked? I touched my chest and closed my eyes, feeling inside of myself like Lucifer had taught me a few days ago.

"The bond is still there," he said, strange relief still dripping from his every word.

I could see it, the glowing thread leading from me to him. So I'd gone through all of that for nothing?

Of course I had, because nothing was fair in Hell. Bitterness flooded me.

The only thing certain was my resolve — I had to escape before my time truly came. Whatever I'd thought we shared, it was ashes now.

*T*he next day, I walked the palace halls in a daze with Mara chattering beside me. My body still ached, but there didn't seem to be any lasting damage. A small relief in my pit of misery.

Usually, I enjoyed Mara's outlandish retellings. Now, I barely heard her animated chatter.

I mechanically nodded and responded at what I hoped were appropriate points, my eyes scanning every corridor we passed. There had to be a way out.

Mara's laughter echoed through the halls as she recounted a particularly scandalous liaison between two demons. I forced a smile, trying to keep up the appearance of interest, but my mind was a whirlwind of confusion and fear.

"Are you listening?" she asked, exasperation filling her tone.

"Hmm? Yeah, yeah, scandalous demons and all that. Riveting," I said, lacking my usual bite.

"You haven't made one crack about Lilith running a frat house." She narrowed her eyes. "Something's off with you. Spill."

I sighed, running a hand through my dishevelled hair. Had I brushed it today?

"It's complicated. I need to figure some things out."

"Complicated? You're in Hell, darling. Everything's complicated," she said with a smirk, her yellow eyes glinting.

She wasn't wrong. Hell was a maze of complications, and I was stuck at the centre of it, searching for a way out.

Where did I start? With the Devil? The soulbond? The ritual? There was too much to unpack, and every time I tried , my jumbled feelings came out stilted and half-finished.

I sighed instead of trying to answer, glancing anywhere but at her. A faint glimmer caught my eye from a door up ahead. I paused, squinting at the sliver of light. Strange — the Citadel's halls didn't usually shine. The vibe here was more doom and gloom.

"Ooh, I've never seen a glowing door in Hell before." Mara clapped her clawed hands together.

Before I could respond, she eagerly skipped towards the door. I hurried to catch up but she reached the door first and threw it open. Blinding white light seared our eyes and for a second I wondered if I'd been hit by Lucifer's spell again. But there was no pain so I dismissed that quickly.

When my vision cleared, a cracked but strangely pristine stairwell appeared before me. Mara leaned in, glancing up without leaving the doorway. She whistled.

"It just keeps going."

Could it be?

The stairs were different than any I'd seen before. Uneven and almost... twisted. Yet something in my bones resonated at the sight of them.

She tilted her head, studying the carved symbols on the wall that resembled ancient druidic runes. "Huh."

I glanced between her and the carvings, a thread of excitement blooming inside of me. "Huh? What's huh?"

"This is it! The Stairway I was talking about weeks ago." She shook her head, chuckling almost deliriously.

I blinked, stunned. "You're sure?"

"Without a doubt. See this mark? That's the signature for Anu's power and he created the Stairway." Her voice took on a hushed, reverent tone. "Never thought I'd see it."

I stared at the stairs, my feet itching to take them. In an ideal world, I would wait and recover more before attempting to escape.

After two weeks, I'd wandered every hallway of this place with Mara or Lucifer by my side. I had never seen this door. If I didn't act now, would I ever find it again?

And if I stayed, what future awaited but death after birthing Lucifer's heir?

No, it had to be now.

"Whoa, hold up there!" Mara said, grabbing my arm before I could step onto the landing beyond the doorway. "I know reckless decisions are your speciality, but we don't know if that thing is stable."

I shook her off, my eyes fixed on the winding steps. "I have to try. This could be my only chance."

Before she could argue further, I stepped onto the landing and planted my foot on the first stair. The stone creaked under my weight but held. I took another tentative step up.

"I'm not joking, get back here!" she shouted. "That thing looks ready to collapse!"

But I was deaf to her warnings, my focus narrowed to single-minded determination.

Survive first, worry later.

One step, then another.

I blocked out Mara's increasingly panicked shouts.

On the sixth stair, the stone fell away beneath my foot and my heart slammed against my rib cage. I quickly moved up a step, knees shaking, narrowly missing a nasty fall.

That was way too close for comfort.

"Mara!" I called over my shoulder. "What's down there if I fall?"

"What do you mean *if* you fall?" Her tone dripped with suspicion.

"Just answer the question."

"What do I look like? A mystical encyclopaedia?" she shouted back, her sarcastic panicked voice echoing around me. "My best guess, the Soul Nexus. It exists in every realm just like the Stairway."

I shuddered. Well, shit. I did not have a swan dive into raw soul energy on my bingo card for the day.

The winding steps disappeared into endless white mist above. I couldn't see the state of the stairs around the bend, let alone whether there was another door nearby.

What if the nearest door isn't for sixty steps?

That was a weirdly specific number. But it was a valid and unnerving concern. Could the stairs support me long enough to reach it?

But going back wasn't an option. It couldn't be. I had to keep going and have faith that I'd make it. Though knowing how The Morrigan had messed with my life, I wasn't sure which god or goddess I was meant to have faith in anymore.

I made it three more steps before the next crack sounded. Only this one was so loud it echoed like a gunshot.

"What in the Seven Circles was that?" Mara shouted, panic ruling her more than me.

I didn't answer her, couldn't. The floor fell out from beneath me.

CHAPTER NINETEEN

LUCIFER

"*W*hy did you summon me?"

She turned to me, eyes wide and wet. "Bronwyn." She pointed at the open door, barely able to get words out in her panic.

My witch had stumbled across the Realm Stairway.

"How did you find this?"

It should have been undetectable to anyone other than those connected to the Core and those who shared blood with the old gods.

Before Mara could respond, a bloodcurdling scream rent the air.

Bronwyn!

My heart seized.

I unfurled my wings and dove into the stairway without hesitation.

Up ahead, three rows of steps had fallen away, leaving an almost impassable gap in the stairs. I tucked my wings and dove in, snapping them out the second I cleared the stone and fell into the white mist of the Soul Nexus.

My power unfurled, creating an automatic barrier between me and the searching tendrils of the Nexus. Bronwyn wouldn't have any such protection from being absorbed.

Cursing, I tucked my wings again and fell with unnatural speed, heart pounding and fear choking me.

When I get her out of this, she's not leaving my sight for a century. Minimum.

The Devil never feared and yet, I'd experienced abject terror twice in two days because of this woman.

Breath whooshed out of me when she appeared in the mist, but I didn't dare hope yet.

My wings unfurled as I passed her, slowing my descent. Her eyes were tightly closed, her jaw clenched as if she could will her way out of this mess.

"You'll be the death of me, witch." My arms wrapped around her slender frame. I pulled her tight to my chest, her body trembling against mine.

My power expanded to protect her from the Nexus as her eyes flew open and she gasped.

"Oh my goddess, Lucifer!" She clung to me, her arms wrapping around my neck. She buried her head in the crook of my shoulder, sobbing, her body shaking against mine.

"Hush. I've got you," I murmured, emotion choking me. Bone-deep relief warred with heart-stopping terror inside me.

She was safe, for now, in my arms, but I had come so close to losing her forever.

We had cut this far too close. If I'd been but a moment later...

My wings beat furiously as I carried us up. Using my power, I blew a bigger hole in the stairs, taking out most of the landing and creating a gap big enough to fit through.

My relief took a back seat once my feet touched the ground of the Infernal Throne. Fury replaced it, boiling in my veins.

"What were you thinking? You could have died!" My grip tightened on her at the thought of it. She flinched and I forced a calmer tone. "Do you know what that would have done to me?"

Her lips parted, but only a sob emerged. My anger melted away. I folded her in my arms, cocooning her in my wings, blocking out our surroundings, and Mara, who had slid down a wall to stare at us, relief blanketing her features.

I held her close as I moved through the halls of my domain, my strides large and rushed. Her tears soaked into my shirt and she trembled while fear and relief warred within me.

I controlled everything here. I had taken great pains to ensure that no demon, creature or being could harm her. And yet, she'd nearly died. Twice.

The realisation was maddening.

Me, the all-powerful Lucifer, incapable of protecting one mortal witch.

It was unconscionable and the exact opposite of what my clamouring instincts demanded. My entire being wanted to keep her safe and close. Instead, I had almost lost her again, this foolish, reckless witch who had somehow become my entire world.

"Why?" I asked when I trusted myself to speak. I peeled my wing away and glanced down at her, still clinging to me. "Why risk yourself so recklessly?"

She shook her head, refusing to meet my eyes. Carefully I grasped her chin, tilting her face up to mine.

"Please, talk to me," I whispered. "Is being here with me truly so abhorrent you'd rather die?"

At that her eyes widened, shimmering with unshed tears. "I had to try…"

"Try what? To kill our unborn daughter?'

Shock rippled across her face. "Daughter?" she breathed.

I nodded.

"H— how do you know?"

"I sensed her when I forced you back to life yesterday."

A brief smile crossed Bronwyn's face, a sight that made my chest ache. A second later, it twisted into a scowl and she struggled in my arms. "Put me down."

"Never again." I held her tighter.

"Lucifer." Her voice dropped in warning.

I turned a corner, oddly relieved to see the doors to my wing.

"No. You cannot be trusted with either of your lives."

She snorted. "Pot meet kettle."

I frowned. "What is that supposed to mean?"

"You're the one who tried to kill me." She shook her head. "If anyone values my life, it's me."

I stared down at her, utter horror beating through me. "You think I…"

With a sigh, I set her on her feet outside my wing

and stepped back. Bronwyn rounded on me, grey eyes flashing.

"Don't try to feed me some bullshit line, Lucifer." She backed away from me, crossing her arms. "You're the one still trying to find a way to break our bond. I'm not the hypocrite here."

I rubbed my temples, frustration rising as Bronwyn continued glaring at me.

"I'm an idiot, you know? Falling in love with the Devil."

I froze, my infernal heart skipping a beat.

"Believing, even for a moment, that you could feel something beyond your precious agreement with The Morrigan."

Grasping her shoulders, I searched her stormy eyes. "Say that again," I rasped.

She looked bewildered, her eyes searching mine for any hint of deceit. "What?"

"Say it again," I insisted. "Tell me that you love me."

She slapped my hands away. "Why? So you can rub it in my face that you'd rather kill me than live tied to another person?"

"No, Bronwyn," I murmured, my tone pleading. "Because I love you too."

"Love? Spare me." Her laughter rang out, a bitter,

incredulous sound. "When you love someone, you don't try to kill them by needlessly severing a soulbond."

"I only tried so that you could choose me for yourself."

She stared at me, her brow furrowing. "W-what?"

I scrubbed a hand across my face, groaning while the disconcerting burn of embarrassment stung my cheeks. Who knew I could actually feel such an emotion?

"I needed to know that you'd choose me, without The Morrigan's influence." I winced as she continued to stare at me, slack-jawed. "Contrary to popular belief, free will is important to me."

Her expression softened but still she said nothing and concern began to gnaw at me.

"Last night…" My voice faltered as the memories of holding her lifeless body resurfaced. I cupped her face gently, staring into her eyes and willing her to hear me. "Last night was the worst thing I've ever endured. Watching you die, hearing your heartbeat stop, knowing that I might lose you forever." Her eyes widened and my eyes narrowed, my tone hardening, "Yes, you died."

Her mouth opened and closed, horror flitting across her face.

"When I thought I'd lost you…" I swallowed hard.

"I never want to experience that again. I love you, Bronwyn, and now I'm so terrified of losing you I don't want to let you out of my sight."

My voice dropped to a husky whisper. "But I see now how ridiculous that was. I cannot lose you and it will be a very long time before I can bear to be away from you, my love."

A single tear slid down her cheek as she searched my gaze. "Do you mean that?" she breathed.

"With all that I am." I pressed my forehead to hers, raw emotion choking me. "Forgive me for making you doubt it even for a moment."

Her lips found mine in answer, a promise and forgiveness. I crushed her close, profoundly grateful for this gift I never deserved — her trust, her heart. I would spend an eternity proving myself worthy of her.

Starting with the surprise in my living room.

CHAPTER TWENTY

BRONWYN

I let Lucifer sweep me into his arms again without protest, still reeling. He loved me. The Devil wanted me by his side forever. Me, the witch who was more likely to set her hair on fire than be the object of anyone's affections.

It was... a lot to process.

I glanced up at his face, those mesmerising blue eyes so warm whenever they rested on me. How had I missed it?

Lucifer carried me through the shadowy halls of his wing in comfortable silence.

"Are you up for some company, petal?" he asked as we approached his living room.

Company? Mara had just left us, so who could he mean?

Lucifer nudged the door open with his shoulder and nodded to the room with his lips quirked in a smug smile. There, perched casually on the sofa, was my grandmother Rowena.

"Gran!"

Lucifer set me gently on my feet and I flew across the room, tackling her in a hug. She laughed, rocking back from the force of it.

"There's my girl," she said, cupping my cheek. I blinked back fresh tears.

"But — how?" I looked between her and Lucifer, bewildered.

He gave a slow smile. "I located her soul in the Summerlands. Odd place for a witch, don't you think?"

Gran winked at him slyly. "Have you seen the stock in the Summerlands?" She shivered, a delighted but unnerving smile on her face. "You didn't think I'd end up in one of the hells, did you?"

I rolled my eyes at her typical nonchalance. "Stock? Really, Gran?"

She chuckled, patting my cheek fondly. Then she

pulled back, studying my face intently. Her eyes narrowed.

"You've been crying." She brushed away the remnants of tears on my lashes.

I winced. I'd done nothing but cry for the last hour. Understanding lit Gran's face. "I see you fulfilled The Morrigan's contract after all." She smirked at Lucifer. "So tell me, Devil. Are you making an honest woman of my granddaughter? Or do we need to have words?"

Lucifer laughed, his amusement genuine. "You would have to destroy me to prevent me from tying Bronwyn to me in every way known to man and immortal."

I blinked, stunned by his words. Had he just... promised to marry me? Was he serious?

Gran let out a delighted cackle. She glanced between us, a sly smile playing on her lips. "That's quite the commitment, Devil. Are you sure you're ready for it?"

Lucifer's eyes remained locked on mine, a solemn intensity in his gaze. "More than you know."

I swallowed hard, emotion choking me yet again. This was going to get old fast.

Her smile turned sad and she reached for my hands, drawing all of my focus to her. "I'm sorry I couldn't prepare you properly, Bron. When The

Morrigan gives an order, it's impossible to refuse, even when you know it could hurt your loved ones."

I blinked in surprise. "What do you mean?"

Gran sighed. "Our magic comes from her. Disobeying would've meant losing it or our minds. That's why your mother left you with me." Pain flashed in her eyes. "She fought the call for thirteen years, but then you came into your power and she couldn't do it anymore. It drove her insane. Not long after she left you in my care, she took her own life."

My throat tightened, chest aching. "She killed herself?"

She nodded, grief etched on her face. "Our ancestor disregarded her children's wellbeing to further her own agenda, whatever it may be."

Lucifer had gone very still. "Ancestor?" he asked.

Gran gave him an incredulous look, as if he were a child who couldn't grasp a simple concept. "The Morrigan, of course."

Surprise flickered across Lucifer's expression, chased by outrage. "Of course. Why else specify an Owen witch bear my heir?" He cursed viciously. "She's scheming her way out of her cage."

I had been nothing but a pawn to her. My mother, my grandmother, myself — manipulated all our lives. But no more. I would not let a goddess dictate my life.

Taking his hands, I met his troubled gaze. "Whatever she has planned, it doesn't matter. I have you now, and Gran, and our daughter. I don't need or want anything else and I won't be her puppet ever again."

Unease and frustration lingered in his gaze. "You can't know that." He pulled me to him and cupped my cheeks, a sad smile claiming his lips. "You're no match for The Morrigan, my love."

I refused to let fear of a vengeful goddess wreck our happiness. Not when I'd had to die twice to get it.

"I'm not naive, I know that, but that doesn't change anything." I placed my hand over his where it rested on my cheek. "Don't you see? Her power over me is finished. She wanted Hell to have an heir, it's getting one. But that's where her involvement ends. If she wants our daughter, she'll have to go through us both."

Lucifer searched my face, then cracked a crooked smile. "Look at you, ready to battle deities for our child's sake." His pride warmed me. "Very well, she will find we are not such easy prey." He ducked his head until our foreheads touched. "Together, there is nothing we cannot overcome, my rebellious queen."

His eyes sparkled with a mixture of affection and desire. I smiled and tilted my chin up to brush a soft kiss over his lips.

"There's nowhere in this world or any other I'd rather be than by your side."

He tightened his grip around me, pulling me closer, deepening the kiss. The taste of him, a bittersweet blend of power and passion, left me breathless and yearning for more.

For a blissful moment, nothing else existed but us.

"Oh, for pity's sake, stop rubbing it in." Rowena huffed, though her eyes twinkled merrily. "Get a room why don't you!"

Laughing, Lucifer pulled back and lifted my hand to brush his lips over my knuckles. He released me reluctantly to turn back to my grandmother.

"Speaking of which, allow me to show you to your new chambers, Rowena."

She flushed. "Well really, Your Darkness, you needn't go to any trouble on my account…"

Lucifer offered an arm to my grandmother with a theatrical flourish. Gran winked at me over her shoulder before they left, leaving me alone with my thoughts.

I traced my fingers over my lips, still tingling from our kiss, shaking my head in wonder. How could life have changed so completely in just a few short weeks?

The all-consuming grief and despair had left me, leaving only joy and optimism in the blink of an eye.

And I wouldn't change a moment of this wild, unexpected journey. Not when it led me here, to love and family and hope.

I glanced around Lucifer's lavish living room. Would I ever get used to calling a place like this home? To calling Hell home? But with Lucifer and Gran here, it already felt more welcoming than anywhere I'd lived before.

No more lonely nights spent wondering why I didn't fit in anywhere. No more keeping everyone at arm's length because somehow they always ended up leaving. I finally had people who wanted me around for the long haul.

It was still hard to believe Lucifer was one of those people.

The actual King of Hell wanted me by his side forever. Me, the messed up witch who never followed rules or did what she was told.

For the first time in years, the future appeared bright, full of possibility. I had a family again. Soon I'd have a daughter, a little piece of both of us to love.

We'd figure the rest out together. As long as I had Lucifer and Gran, I could handle anything this twisted underworld threw at me. This was where I belonged.

CHAPTER TWENTY-ONE

LUCIFER

"*C*an we do something about the burning demons on the lawn?"

A week had passed since I saved Bronwyn from yet another death. Now that we weren't trying to break the bond, life had become much easier. Even with her grandmother breathing down my neck, dropping hints as sharp as a hellhound's teeth about weddings, and pestering every male guard in the citadel.

It was… nice. A change of pace I hadn't expected to want, but I'd quickly started looking forward to our family dinners and my private magical training sessions with Brownyn.

Still, the craving refused to let up. At this point, I spent most of my waking moments consumed with the need to sink my teeth into her and bind us together in a way I'd never wanted before.

"Are you even listening to me, Lucie?" Bronwyn shouted.

My attention snapped to her with an apologetic wince. She stared at me, jaw clenched in frustration and her hands on her hips.

"Apologies, love. My mind was elsewhere." I approached her, smiling as her eyes narrowed. "But I'm listening now. What were you saying about the lawn?"

We stood in the heart of my private training rooms, a space I'd fortified with magic so dense that even the most catastrophic loss of control wouldn't damage the rest of the citadel.

She huffed, crossing her arms over her chest. "The pyres. They're a bit... morbid for the front garden, don't you think?" She eyed me with suspicion as I drew closer. Considering we had been running through scenarios to extradite her from a close-contact attack, I couldn't blame her. "The smoke is wafting into the citadel and making me nauseous. I don't care how willing they are, there's something about the idea of someone torturing themselves for eternity to make a point that turns my stomach."

Ah, the Eternal Pyres. "I suppose we could tone down the eternal damnation aesthetic a bit," I mused, watching her reaction closely.

Bronwyn's annoyance was clear, yet there was a playful spark in her eyes that I found captivating. "A bit?" she echoed, her tone laden with sarcasm. "How about completely? It's not exactly welcoming, you know."

I kept reminding her that Hell wasn't meant to be welcoming. It hadn't stuck yet.

"Alright, I'll talk to the Council of Lords about relocating them further from the citadel. The denizens of Hell have become rather attached to their symbol of devotion."

"More like a dramatic declaration of masochism," she muttered beneath her breath before forcing her shoulders to relax. "Thank you. I appreciate it."

I bit the inside of my cheek, fighting back a chuckle that she wouldn't appreciate. "Perhaps we'll replace them with a nice fountain instead?" I teased, moving closer to her.

The shift in her expression was immediate, her annoyance melting into amusement. "A fountain of fire, maybe?" she shot back, matching my step with a backwards retreat. Her back hit the wall of the training room, the magical runes etched into the stone glowing softly under her touch.

I leaned in, my hands on either side of her, trapping her in the space between my arms. "Only the best for my queen," I murmured, the proximity bringing a fresh wave of that maddening desire to the surface.

For a moment, we simply looked at each other, the air charged with the tension that always seemed to crackle between us. Then, without thinking, I closed the distance, capturing her lips with mine.

Bronwyn's initial shock gave way to a burning need that matched my own as she kissed me back, her hands finding their way into my hair, pulling me closer. The kiss deepened, driven by a hunger that had everything to do with the soul-deep connection we shared.

When we finally parted, breathless and more entangled than before, her forehead rested against mine. "Lucifer," she whispered, her voice a mix of reprimand and affection. "You were supposed to be helping me control my magic, not... whatever this is."

I chuckled, unable to resist brushing a kiss against her forehead. "I'd argue this is a form of control. Just not the kind we had planned on practising today."

She pushed against my chest, a futile effort to create distance. "You're impossible," she said, though the warmth in her voice belied her words.

"Only for you," I admitted, stepping back to grant her the space she sought but not the distance.

Bronwyn eyed me warily. "No more kissing until I've mastered at least one spell without blowing something up."

I tried to step back, I really did. But some age-old instinct took a firm grip. My gaze fixed on her neck, the pulse there beating a tantalising rhythm that sang to the very core of my being.

The desire to mark and claim her as mine burned through me, primal and unrelenting. I shook myself, trying to clear the haze of need. This wasn't something to be taken lightly.

"I don't think I can agree to that," I said, my voice barely above a whisper.

Her eyes, wide and a little wary, met mine. "Why?"

"I've been... experiencing a… need." I struggled to find words that wouldn't frighten her. "An intense need to…" I swallowed, "bite you."

I searched her face, waiting for her to recoil in disgust but willing her to understand the gravity of this.

To my surprise, she laughed — a light, disbelieving chuckle. "Bite me? Like a vampire bite?" She seemed more amused than scared, which wasn't the reaction I'd expected.

"Not exactly." I took a deep breath, trying to steady

myself. "Angels form permanent bonds through a mating ritual unlike anything mortals practise. If I were to bite you, it would irrevocably tie you to me in every way — body, mind, and soul."

Surprise flickered in her eyes, followed by consideration.

"More than The Morrigan already has?" Her smirk was back, that fearless challenge that always drew me closer.

"More permanently than *any* contract or spell." I frowned at her. Why wasn't she running scared? "It would link our lifespans, extend yours to match mine. You'd always know where I am, and I you. It's a bond that not even death could easily break." I cupped her cheek, thumb stroking over her soft skin. "I've fought it since Inferna but it's getting stronger. It's no small thing to ask of you."

"Nothing about our relationship has been small." She turned her face into my touch, pressing a kiss to my palm that sent a shudder through me. "I made a deal with the Devil, got dragged to Hell, impregnated, and somewhere along the way, found myself falling in love with you. I'm in this for the long haul, Lucifer. However you want to seal that promise, I'm ready."

Then her expression softened, her amusement

fading into something more contemplative. "But do you really want this?" she asked in a quiet voice.

"I do." The conviction in my own tone surprised me. "I never thought I'd want it, I never felt the need and at some point I must have written it off as a myth. But I can't fight it anymore. It's... it's not just about desire, petal. It's about choosing you, for all eternity."

A moment passed, heavy with decision. Then, slowly, she nodded. "Okay. Yes."

Elation swept through me and I drew her against me, my arms wrapping around her waist, pulling her close. Our bodies melted together as if they were two pieces of a puzzle, fitting perfectly. I claimed her lips again and the room disappeared, replaced by an explosion of desire that overwhelmed me.

Her lips were soft, inviting, and tasted like sweet ambrosia. The kiss deepened, our tongues duelling in a dance I never wanted to end. Her heart pounded against my chest, matching the rhythm of my own. My hands roamed her body, exploring every familiar curve and contour, luxuriating in this unexpected reality.

I'd had aeons to come to terms with the fact that I would one day be a father. Never, in all the time, did I think I'd find someone as accepting as Bronwyn, someone who would challenge me at every turn.

She clung to me, matching my intensity with a

fervour that left me shaken. My need grew, her small gasps of pleasure urging me on. She whispered my name like a prayer as I devoured her mouth, my body fitting against hers with a familiar desperation.

In the heat of the moment, I let my power slip, allowing it to flow around us. It caressed her, brushing against her sensitive skin in ways that made me ache. Her clothes melted away under my touch, leaving her naked and vulnerable.

She gasped, pulling away from the kiss, her eyes wide with surprise, but also amusement. "Why do we need to be naked for you to bite me?"

I grinned, my eyes roaming over her naked form. "It's more fun this way," I said, my voice husky with desire.

I pressed her against the wall of the training room, the runes glowing softly under our touch. I lifted her with ease and she wrapped her legs around my waist, pulling me closer. Her heat, her desire, all of it flowed through me, fuelling my own.

With a thought, my clothes joined hers in the ether. My hard cock grazed her opening and we both groaned. Need burned in her eyes, mirroring my own. Frustration built that I didn't have more hands to drive her higher… and then the perfect idea hit.

My power stopped caressing her. Instead, it gripped

her, supporting her against the wall, the pulse of it undulating against her sensitive skin in a way that made her moan.

I released my grip on her and took my cock in hand, grinning as her eyes glazed over at the sight.

"Are you ready for me, petal?"

She nodded, swallowing as I dragged the swollen head back and forth along her slick folds, teasing her, testing her. Each time I grazed her clit, she shuddered, her nails digging into my shoulders. She kept trying to pull me closer, to force me inside of her, but I resisted, enjoying the promise of what was to come.

"Stop messing around, Lucifer," she growled, her eyes flashing with impatience and desire. "I'm ready."

I grinned, unable to resist teasing her a little longer. She arched her back, her hips bucking against mine and I couldn't deny her any longer.

I'm not sure I'll ever be able to deny her again.

Her wetness coated my length as I thrust into her with one swift thrust, filling her completely. The feeling of her around me was intoxicating, always would be. It drove me to the brink of madness.

She moaned, her head falling back against the wall, exposing her neck to me. I couldn't resist the temptation. I kissed her pulse, my teeth grazing her skin, teasing her. She shuddered, her nails digging into my shoulders.

I began to move, each thrust driving us both closer to the edge.

The room around us faded away, replaced by the sound of our pants and the slap of skin against skin. The bond between us twisted, digging deeper as it grew stronger again and I lost all semblance of control. I slammed into her, desperate to feel her falling over the edge so I could finally sink my teeth into her.

With a singular determination, I drove into her harder and harder, grinding against her clit any chance I got. When her inner walls tightened, and her body stiffened against me, I quickened my pace, my teeth aching in anticipation.

"Are you sure?" I asked one last time, my lips brushing against her skin.

"Yes," she whispered back, her hand moving to the back of my head, a silent encouragement.

With her affirmation echoing in my mind, her breath hitched, and her body convulsed around mine from the intensity of her orgasm, I let the instinct take over. My teeth extended, sharper than any human's could ever be, and I bit down gently at first, then with a firmness that sealed the pact. The taste of her flooded my senses, sweet and powerful. The magic of the bite weaved around us, a second golden thread binding our souls together.

She gasped at the rush of power, then melted into me with a contented sigh. I cradled her close, awed by the new, profound connection between us. We were mated by choice, two souls entwined for all eternity.

I pulled away, licking the blood from my lips. She stared up at me, her eyes glazed with pleasure, a satisfied smile playing on her lips. She reached up, touching the mark on her neck with a sense of wonder.

"How do you feel?" I asked when I found my voice again.

She pursed her lips, thinking. "Stronger. Like I could take on the world." Her eyes closed and then she smiled. "I can sense you, here. More than before." She touched her chest over her heart.

I covered her hand with mine. "You honour me by accepting this gift, petal." I brushed back her hair, tenderness swelling within me.

Her eyes opened, shining with amusement and love. "Does this mean I can beat you in a fight now if I really try?"

I chuckled. "I wouldn't go that far, little witch. But you'll find your magic much easier to control."

Bronwyn grinned. "Good."

Unable to resist, I pulled her close for a searing kiss,

revelling in our new connection. For some reason, it felt so much more real than The Morrigan's soulbond. Maybe because it hadn't taken a contract to trick her into tying herself to me.

She had chosen me this time.

I intended to spend the rest of our long lives thanking her for that.

EPILOGUE

THE MORRIGAN

Two years later
Somewhere else...

The revellers danced and drank, their laughter grating. How I envied their ignorance. Trapped as we were, they carried on as if naught were amiss. Fools. Did they not feel the stagnation seeping into their immortal bones?

I shifted upon my onyx throne, ignoring the sharp edge digging into my thigh. Let it bite me. The pain gave focus. And I needed my wits to maintain the illusion — The Morrigan, unconcerned by her confinement.

Your self-imposed *confinement.*

None must suspect the bitter truths. That boredom and despair warred within me daily. That I yearned to walk the earth once more, to stretch my wings and indulge in the mortals' petty wishes. The aching void left by my severed connection to the witches and their intoxicating prayers.

Centuries of meticulous planning undone thanks to traitors with overinflated egos. My spell was meant to block Ethereorium, the god realm, from the other eight in our world. My warriors were meant to be walking free, dispatching traitors and cleaning house on Earth. Instead, they were trapped between the veil when the Witches Council betrayed their own kind.

So many pieces had been left to the council of idiots I had appointed ready for my prolonged absence. They had orders. They knew what my visions predicted, yet they dragged their feet. And for what? Fear of sharing their power?

I should have picked better.

Why didn't I include an exemption in the spell?

The reality of what confinement would mean hadn't settled in my bones until I found myself locked within my court, watching my idiot brethren waste all of their power raging at the barrier blocking us. My court powered me, but there was only so much they could do for the insistent boredom.

Their delays were entertaining for a time, but as the centuries wore on, they became glaringly short-sighted. They claimed to understand the need to restore balance, but the longer they pussyfooted around the subject, making nothing but empty gestures and promises, the more the natural order felt our absence.

Fractures formed in the other realms, and the foolish Kings scrambled to fill them, pulling more power each time, risking their lives to shore up something easily fixed if they would *just* listen to me.

Yet even a crisis could not unite them. They continued squabbling like children over dwindling spoils. Fearful of the repercussions if one of them pulled more power. What if Hades pulled more power than Nyxandra and then tried to take Irkalla from her?

They argued for decades, possibly a century, over the rules they should impose to maintain order amongst themselves. One partner? Three? Where would they draw the line?

I'd given up intervening fifty years into my confinement. Once I had tried to guide them toward reconciliation as I guided so many rulers of old. But bitterness choked my counsel. Let them exhaust themselves in petty conflicts. When my warriors freed themselves from the veil, they would crawl to me, and I would remember how they scorned my aid after the seals closed.

Only Lucifer had changed the status quo.

My crystal ball appeared before me, the glass swirling with mist and untold distractions. I reached for it, my pulse quickening as it settled with a happy buzz of energy in my palm. The mist cleared, revealing Lucifer and the witch I had chosen for him. I should have been insulted that he thought he could resist the gift of my own flesh and blood, but his fight had kept me entertained for a short while.

He crawled on the floor, the key to fixing the balance in the Netherrealm bouncing on his back, giggling happily. Her fiery red curls bounced as she shrieked orders at him while my great-however-many-grands granddaughter sat nearby smirking.

She had a right to that smirk. She didn't realise it, but she had done exactly as I ordered. Reducing the fearsome Lucifer Morningstar to a plaything for a toddler was just a bonus.

Yes, it annoyed me that it had taken longer than I had planned. However, it still impressed me that her ancestors had evaded him for so long. Three centuries was a long time to go without making a power sacrifice.

But finally. The pieces were starting to fall into place.

As I had predicted, with Lucie gaining his heir, the others scrambled to keep pace, terrified of falling behind as he grew in strength. Excitement fizzled beneath my skin as I watched the other Kings and Queens scramble in panic first at Bronwyn's coronation and then at the birth of the first Morningstar child. Unease, outrage, fear. It all rippled on the currents of time, delicious and entertaining all at once

Maliwen's birth brought me one step closer to freeing The Twelve. One step closer to wrecking bloody havoc on the Witches Council who had grown lazy over the last three hundred years.

I cared not how much blood flowed to return power to my loyal witches. Only that it happened.

And little Maliwen would play her part in that.

Bronwyn thought her role was complete and believed herself beyond my influence. Balance would be restored precisely as I willed and not even my granddaughter's stubbornness would stand in my way.

The real fun was about to begin.

I hope you enjoyed Infernal Bargain.

This story quite literally came out of nowhere. I saw a meme, loved it but had no ideas. Then six months later it hit me so hard that I couldn't stop writing until it was done. It was exactly what I needed in that moment and I sincerely hope it was what you needed too.

If you're like me, the end is never enough. Subscribe to my newsletter and grab a sneak peek at Hell's version of a baby and bridal shower.

NEXT UP

Next up is Bound By The Goddess.

When the Goddess of War and Witchcraft decides to play matchmaker, you know things are gonna get messy.

I was used to my fire magic causing trouble, but three mysterious strangers ignited something in me I'd never felt before. An eternal Soul Bond gifted by The Morrigan herself, tying me to Knox, Finlay and Rhydian forever.

As witches, keeping magic hidden from humans is key. But there's nothing subtle about these three men, or the way they make me feel. Soon our passion and powers are spiralling out of control.

We have to master the depth of the Bond before we lose each other... or end up on the front page of the tabloids. 'Cause one thing's for sure — when The Morrigan wants to stir up chaos, she doesn't do it by half measures.

This witch has her work cut out for her. But with three irresistible heroes by my side? Bring on the madness.

CONTENT ADVISORIES

Tropes:

Forced Proximity. Mild Enemies to Lovers. Accidental (but really not) Pregnancy. Soul mate bond. Resisting Fate. Magical Coercion. Breeding. Fast Burn. Fish out of water. Devil/Witch.

Triggers:

Kidnapping. Violence. Mutual Dubious Consent, forced into sexual relations via a lust spell created by an ancient Goddess. Sexual content. Pregnancy. Death (on and off page).

ABOUT SELINA

Selina Bevan is a British paranormal romance author who writes delicious heroes and captivating worlds, delving deep into the magic and love, with witches, deities, and a spectrum of supernatural beings finding their soulmates in the most unexpected places.

She is a chai tea addict who loves a good gig and finding new alt-rock music when mindlessly scrolling Instagram at night.

Selina writes MF and RH/Why Choose romances with strong-willed but flawed British heroines.